"Did yo... ...at I could me... ...er and then walk away from her again?"

A lump ballooned in Daisy's throat. Nothing would come between Alessio and his desire to win his daughter's affection.

"You are about to play a leading role in fulfilling our daughter's painfully obvious desire for a *real* family."

Her violet eyes were strained. "I'm more than willing to meet you halfway for Tara's sake. You can see her whenever you like."

"I expect much more than that from you."

"What are your terms?"

"I've made the decision that will best serve all our needs. We will get married again."

LYNNE GRAHAM was born in Northern Ireland and has been a keen romance reader since her teens. She is very happily married with an understanding husband, who has learned to cook since she started to write! Her three children keep her on her toes. She has a very large Old English sheepdog who knocks everything over, and two cats. When time allows, Lynne is a keen gardener.

Books by Lynne Graham

Don't miss any of our special offers. Write to us at the following address for information on our newest releases.

Harlequin Reader Service
U.S.: 3010 Walden Ave., P.O. Box 1325, Buffalo, NY 14269
Canadian: P.O. Box 609, Fort Erie, Ont. L2A 5X3

LYNNE GRAHAM

Second-Time Bride

Harlequin Books

TORONTO • NEW YORK • LONDON
AMSTERDAM • PARIS • SYDNEY • HAMBURG
STOCKHOLM • ATHENS • TOKYO • MILAN
MADRID • WARSAW • BUDAPEST • AUCKLAND

ISBN 0-373-11888-0

SECOND-TIME BRIDE

First North American Publication 1997.

Copyright © 1997 by Lynne Graham.

CHAPTER ONE

TARA stood in the doorway, a daunting five feet nine inches of teenage truculence. 'Why do I have to go to Aunt Janet's?'

'Because that's what you do on Saturdays if I have to work.' Daisy shimmied her slender hips into a burgundy skirt while frantically trying to do up her blouse with her other hand, one anxious eye on her daughter, the other on the clock by the bedside. 'And if you're at Janet's I don't have to worry about you.'

'Yeah, so, like, it's not for *my* benefit, it's for *yours*.' Dark brown eyes rested accusingly on her much smaller parent.

'Look, can we have this out tonight?' Daisy begged, feverishly digging through the foot of her wardrobe for two matching shoes.

'I'm thirteen and I'm not stupid. I wouldn't drink or do drugs—'

'I should hope not,' Daisy muttered with a compulsive shudder.

'And I'm not like you were. I'm really sensible and mature for my age—'

'Why do I sometimes get the impression that I'm no giant in your opinion?'

'Mum, you're bound to be a worrier! You got taken in and rolled out by a major creep at seventeen and you've been paying for it ever since because you got stuck with me,' Tara reminded her ruefully. 'But I am not going to make the same mistake. Unless Mr Impossibly-

Rich-and-Handsome comes knocking on the door while you're out, you're safe! I just want to go down to the market with Susie and buy a new top. All the best things will be gone if I have to wait until this afternoon—'

'I have *never* felt stuck with you!' Daisy protested.

'Mum...we haven't got time to get into that sort of stuff. The market?' Tara pleaded.

Daisy hurried through the gilded glass doors of Elite Estates exactly forty-five minutes later, breathless and feeling harassed but trying not to look it. Her boss, Giles Carter, had phoned first thing to inform her that the virus doing the rounds of the agency had knocked out the boy wonder on the sales team—Barry the Barracuda, as Daisy thought of him in private. Her presence was required to deal with Barry's latest new client on what should have been a much cherished day off.

Daisy had worked ten years for Elite Estates and had no illusions about management chauvinism. She was the token woman on the sales staff. She had fought her way up the office ranks with the greatest difficulty, disadvantaged by her sex, her lack of height and her youthful appearance. It had taken hard sales figures to persuade Giles to take her seriously but he still ensured that she dealt only with the properties at the lowest end of the market.

'Giles has phoned down for you twice,' Joyce on Reception told her in a warning hiss. 'And boy, have you got a treat in store...'

Daisy felt a cold chill down her back. Giles had never given her a treat in his life. She always got the difficult clients. 'It's not that old lady back again, is it? Mrs Sykes?'

Joyce laughed. 'Didn't you notice the limousine out front?'

Daisy had been in too much of a hurry to notice anything. Now she looked and saw the impressive long silver vehicle parked outside.

'The most utterly dreamy-looking guy I've ever seen got out of it,' Joyce sighed in a languishing undertone. 'Sadly, an utterly dreamy-looking blonde got out with him.'

A couple... Hopefully the type who still liked each other and respected each other's opinions. Daisy had had some nightmare experiences with twosomes who hadn't been able to agree on anything when it had come to the home of their dreams. Last-minute pull-outs on sales had been the result.

She knocked on the door of Giles's sumptuous office and walked straight in.

It was the woman she saw first. She was studying her watch with a little *moue* of annoyance, a fabulous mane of corn-gold hair partially concealing her features. A tall dark male was standing with his back turned to the door. He swung fluidly round as Daisy entered but she couldn't see his face in the sunlight flooding through the windows.

Giles gave her an exasperated look. 'I expected you sooner than this,' he complained ungraciously.

'Sorry,' Daisy said to the room at large. 'I hope you haven't been waiting too long.'

'Miss Thornton... this is Mr Leopardi and Miss Nina Franklin.' Giles introduced them in the oily voice he employed solely around wealthy clients.

Daisy froze. *Leopardi*. That name thudded into her brain like a sharp blow. Stunned, she stared at the large male presence now blocking out the sunlight. All she could focus on was a pale blue tie set against a slice of snowy white shirt bounded by the lapels of an exquisitely tailored charcoal-grey jacket. Numbly she tipped her silver-fair head back and looked up at him. Disbelief enclosed her in complete stasis. It *was* Alessio! The shock of recognition was so intense that she couldn't move a muscle. She simply stood there, all colour drained from her triangular face, her polite smile sliding away into nothingness. The hand she had begun to extend dropped weakly back to her side again.

Helplessly she collided with deep-set dark eyes fixed on her with an incredulous intensity that was as great as her own. And then luxuriant black lashes swept low, swiftly screening his gaze from her. She saw the tautness of his facial muscles beneath the gold of his dark skin, grasped the fierce control he was exerting and, with a huge effort, dragged her shattered eyes from him, fighting to regain her composure.

'Mr Leopardi...' she muttered in a wobbly undertone, and began to raise her hand again with all the flair of a malfunctioning automaton.

Alessio ignored the gesture and spun on his heel to address Giles. 'Is this woman the only employee you have available?' he enquired harshly.

There was a sharp little silence.

'Miss Thornton is one of our most experienced members of staff.' Giles fixed an ingratiating smile to his full lips but his dismay was obvious. 'Perhaps you think she seems a little on the young side but she's actually a good deal older than she looks!'

Daisy flushed to the hairline. The beautiful blonde giggled. The thick silence pulsed like a wild thing in a room that now felt suffocatingly airless. She focused on Alessio's shoes—hand-stitched Italian loafers. She remembered him barefoot and in trainers. That was the only thought in her mind but it speedily flowed on into another.

She remembered a teenage boy, *not* a full-grown adult male. She knew the adult only from pictures in newsprint that fractured her peace for days afterwards. But how much more disturbing it was to be faced with Alessio in the flesh...and without any warning whatsoever. Her tummy muscles were horribly cramped up. She felt sick, physically sick, and could not have opened her mouth had her life depended on it.

Giles cleared his throat uneasily. 'I'm afraid that there isn't anyone else available this morning. If it wasn't for *this*—' he frowned down at the clumsy plaster cast on his foot '—I would have been delighted to personally escort you round the Blairden property. As it is—'

'Alessio...if we don't get a move on, I'll be late for my booking,' the blonde complained petulantly, unfolding lithely from her chair to reveal a height very little short of Alessio's six feet three.

The woman was a model—a very well-known model, Daisy recognised belatedly, her dazed eyes scanning that impossibly perfect bone structure. She had seen that same face on countless magazine covers. And what had Giles said her name was? Like a sleepwalker, she moved forward and extended her hand. 'Miss Franklin...'

Manicured fingertips brushed hers only in passing. Bored green eyes flicked dismissively over her. The blonde slid her hand into Alessio's in a gesture of possessive intimacy and curved right round him to whisper something in his ear, her other hand moving caressingly up over his chest to curve finally to one broad shoulder.

Daisy went rigid and stared. Then abruptly she looked away, but every nerve in her body screamed as she did so. For a split second, as her own fingers had closed tightly in on themselves, she had been tempted to thrust their bodies apart. That insane urge shook her inside out.

'If you'll excuse me, I'll brief Miss Thornton.' Giles closed a taut hand round Daisy's elbow and practically pulled her out into the corridor.

His heavy features were flushed and angry. 'What's the silent act in aid of? No wonder the bloke wasn't impressed! Don't you know who he is?'

Daisy studied the wall opposite.

'The Leopardi Merchant Bank...that's who he is! I mean, you just stood there gawking at him! Hell's teeth, why does the richest client we've had in months have to come through the door the one and only day Barry's away sick?' Giles groaned in disbelief.

And it couldn't be happening to a nicer person, Daisy found herself thinking, because it was easier to think about that than to think of what had just happened. Of all the estate agencies in the London area, why had Alessio had to choose this one? Was it because of the grovelling service Giles offered to the well-heeled? Alessio was so rich that he would get that kind of service anywhere. Her temples pounded with sick tension.

'Hey...you're not coming down with this blasted virus *too*, are you?' Giles demanded, taking an almost comically fast step back from her.

'No...' Daisy finally found her voice again. 'I'm fine.'

'Then what's the matter with—?' Giles fell abruptly silent as the door behind her opened.

'Since we're in a hurry, Miss Thornton's services will be adequate,' Alessio asserted flatly.

Goose-flesh prickled along the nape of Daisy's neck. She didn't turn round even though she could see Giles regarding that scarcely civil oversight with a fresh look of incomprehension. *Adequate?* Her teeth clenched. Fierce resentment, backed by a rolling tide of humiliation she didn't want to admit to, flared through her taut length.

Thirteen years ago she had been unceremoniously dumped and she had done nothing to deserve Alessio's brutally dismissive reaction to her in front of her boss and his girlfriend. Was it embarrassment? Or was he, just like her, fighting off a distressing surge of adolescent memories? Don't kid yourself, Daisy, a more cynical voice urged. Even at nineteen, Alessio Leopardi didn't have a sensitive bone in his body...

Rigid-backed, Daisy descended the wrought-iron spiral staircase that ran down to the ground floor, and walked out through the crowded front office. Her legs felt as if they might fold beneath her at any moment. A deep trembling was beginning inside her. Shock was setting in hard. As she emerged out onto the pavement and began turning in the direction of the staff car park, Alessio drawled from behind her, 'We'll use the limo.'

'Of course,' she managed half under her breath.

'So tell us about this house,' Nina Franklin invited thinly as Daisy slid stiffly along the indicated seat opposite her.

Daisy's lips parted and closed again. She knew virtually nothing about the property in Blairden Square, not even if there were any offers on it. Since Giles had never allowed her to deal with what he termed the 'superior residences' on the agency books, she had had no reason to take any interest in them. Starter homes and apartments were generally her field. But had she been in her right mind she would have checked out the facts before she'd left the office.

A glossy brochure landed squarely on her lap. She jumped. Startled violet eyes switched to the male she had been rigorously avoiding looking at.

'Time to bone up,' Alessio said very drily, his expressive mouth as hard as iron.

'You're not very efficient, are you?' his companion remarked in cutting addition. 'High-powered sales routines are painful but total ignorance is something else again!'

Daisy had coloured but she tilted her chin. 'I'm afraid I haven't dealt with this particular property before—'

'It's a Georgian terrace,' Alessio slotted in gently. 'But don't worry about it. We can read too.'

Daisy bent her head, his smooth derision stinging like acid on her over-sensitive skin. Why was he treating her like this? Alessio was blunt but he had never been a boor. She didn't understand his apparent need to humiliate her. Surely he couldn't *still* be blaming her after all these years? And it was so ridiculous to be forced to pretend that they were strangers. Was that her fault... or his? He had made no attempt to acknowledge their previous relationship either. But then why should he have? Why should either of them want to? That relationship was all but lost in the mists of time, she told herself, until intelligence intervened. How could that long-ago summer ever be lost for her when she had Tara? Her stomach cramped again into even tighter knots.

The buzz of a mobile phone broke the tense silence. Daisy didn't lift her head. But she couldn't concentrate, couldn't even begin to study the brochure. It was as if her whole brain had gone into a state of suspended animation, as if the world had stopped dead the instant she'd glanced up and seen Alessio in Giles's office. No longer the long, lean youth she recalled but, if anything, even more heartbreakingly handsome...

He had level dark brows, cheekbones sharp enough to cut concrete, an aristocratic blade of a nose, lustrous tawny eyes and a head of glossy black hair, now ruthlessly suppressed into a smooth cut and infinitely shorter than she recalled. His hard-boned features were intensely male, his wide, beautifully shaped mouth pure sensual threat. He could smile and steal your heart with one scorching, teasing glance... but *that* had been the boy, not the man, Daisy reminded herself painfully.

She flinched as Nina Franklin gave an explosive little shriek of annoyance and thrust the mobile phone back into her capacious bag.

'I can't stay!' she told Alessio furiously. 'Joss needs me now. I could scream but how can I refuse? He's done me too many favours. You might as well let me out here. I can walk to the studio faster than you can get me there in this traffic! Look, I'll try to make it over to the house before you leave.'

'Relax...it's not important,' Alessio murmured soothingly.

'I could strangle Joss!' the blonde exclaimed resentfully, and then her green eyes landed on Daisy and hardened to accusing arrows of steel. 'If *you* had been on time, this wouldn't be happening!'

'Perhaps you would prefer to cancel and make a fresh appointment?' Daisy suggested with an eagerness she couldn't conceal.

'No, I'll keep this one,' Alessio drawled.

Stiff as a small statue, Daisy quite deliberately averted her gaze as the limousine stopped; the other woman slid out, but not without many regretful mutterings and an attempt at a lingering and physical goodbye that had car horns screeching in protest as the lights changed. *Of course* they were lovers. Daisy's fine features were clenched fiercely tight. The intimacy between them was blatant.

Viewing a house together... Were they getting married? Her stomach twisted as she pondered that idea for the first time. For some reason she suddenly felt as if somebody was jumping up and down on her lungs. The door slammed again, sealing her into unwanted isolation with Alessio, and Daisy stopped breathing altogether.

'It's been a day for unpleasant surprises,' Alessio commented grimly.

Daisy finally got up the courage to look at him again, her strained violet eyes unguarded. 'Is that why you felt that you had to take it out on me?'

'You are not one of my happier memories. What did you expect?' Hard eyes regarded her pale face without any perceptible emotion at all.

'I don't know...' Daisy whispered unevenly. 'I just never expected to see you again.'

'Look on this as a once-in-a-lifetime coincidence,' Alessio urged with chilling contempt. 'As greedy little bitches go, you're still top of the list in my experience! I would go some distance to avoid a repeat of this encounter.'

In the pin-dropping silence which ensued, Daisy turned bone-white. Her appalled gaze clung to his set dark features and the cold hostility stamped there. He made no attempt to hide the emotion. Shock rolled over her in a revitalised wave. He despised her; he *really* despised her! But why? Why should he feel like that? Hadn't she let him go free? Hadn't she given him back what he'd wanted and needed and what she should never have taken? Hadn't that single, unselfish action been sufficient to defuse his resentment?

'But it is some consolation to learn that you're now poor enough to be forced to earn a living,' Alessio acknowledged, his cold eyes resting on her like ice-picks in search of cruelly tender flesh.

'I don't understand what you're getting at... I've always worked for a living. And how can you call me a greedy bitch?' Daisy suddenly lashed back at him, shock splintering to give way to angry defensiveness.

Alessio emitted a sardonic laugh, his nostrils flaring. 'Isn't that what you are?'

'In what way was I greedy?' Daisy pressed in ever growing bewilderment. 'I took nothing from you or your family.'

'You call half a million pounds nothing?'

A furrow formed between her delicate brows. 'But I refused the money. Your father tried very hard to make me accept it but I refused.'

'You're a liar.' Alessio's eloquent mouth twisted with derision. 'My father was not the leading light in that deal. You made the demand. He paid up only because he was foolishly trying to protect me.'

'I didn't demand anything... and I didn't accept any money either!' Daisy protested heatedly.

Alessio dealt her a look of complete indifference that cut like a knife. 'I don't even know why I mentioned it. That pay-off was the tacky but merciful end to a very sordid little affair.'

Daisy bit the soft underside of her lower lip and tasted the acrid tang of her own blood. The pain steadied her a little. Alessio's father, Vittorio, had obviously lied. Clearly he had told his son that she *had* accepted the money. And why should that lie surprise her? The

Leopardi clan had loathed her on sight. His parents had tried hard to hide the fact when Alessio was around, but his twin sister, Bianca, had shown her hostility openly. Daisy stared into space, her whole being engulfed by a powerful wave of remembered pain and rejection.

In the swirling oblivion of that tide of memory she relived the heady scent of lush grass bruised by their lovemaking, the kiss of the Tuscan sun on her skin and the passionate weight and urgency of Alessio's lean body on hers. Broken dreams and lost innocence. Her eyes burned, her small frame tensing defensively. Why had nobody ever told her how much loving could hurt and destroy? By the time she had found out that reality, the damage had been done and her reward had been guilt and despair. A 'sordid little affair'? No, for her it had been so much more, and it was in the divergence of outlook that the seeds of disaster had been sown...

The clink of glass dredged her back from her dangerous passage into the past. Her lashes fluttered in confusion as Alessio leant lithely forward and slotted a brandy goblet between her nerveless fingers. 'You look like you are about to pass out.'

Faint colour feathered then into Daisy's drawn cheeks. She watched him help himself to a drink from the cabinet, every movement calm and precise. He did *not* look as though *he* was about to pass out. Although if he ever found out about Tara he might well make good the oversight. Hurriedly, she crushed that disturbing, foolish thought. Alessio had never wanted their baby.

At nineteen, Alessio had been able to think of an awful lot of things he wanted but they had not included a baby. So, knowing that, why on earth had she let him marry her? And yet the answer to that was so simple. She had honestly believed that he loved her...deep down inside...even though he hadn't been showing it any more. It was amazing what a besotted teenage girl could persuade herself to believe, she conceded painfully.

'And you are wearing odd shoes,' Alessio remarked in a curiously flat tone.

A feeling of unreality was starting to enclose Daisy but she also sensed that Alessio was not as in control as he wanted to appear. She surveyed her feet, saw one black court shoe, one navy. It didn't bother her. In the midst of a nightmare encounter, unmatched shoes were a triviality. She drained the brandy in one gulp. It sent fire chasing into the chilled pit of her stomach. She swallowed convulsively. 'I wasn't supposed to be working today. I came out in a hurry.'

'You've cut your hair.'

Daisy lifted an uncertain hand halfway to her shoulder-length bob of shining silver-blonde hair, connected with brilliant eyes and wondered why time seemed to be slowing up, why they were now having this curiously stilted conversation when barely a minute ago they had been arguing. 'Yes. It's easier to manage.'

Alessio was running that narrowed, gleaming gaze over her slight figure in a manner which made her feel incredibly hot and uncomfortable. A wolfish smile gradually curved his hard mouth as he lounged back with innate grace in the seat opposite. 'You don't seem to have much to say to me...'

She wasn't about to tell him that he was still gorgeous. Even as a teenager he had known that and had shamelessly utilised that spectacular combination of smouldering dark good looks and animal sex appeal to his own advantage. He had used it on Daisy—dug his own grave, really, when she thought about it. She had been agonisingly naïve and had fallen like a ton of bricks for him, defenceless against that polished seduction routine of his.

'You're still full of yourself,' Daisy told him helplessly.

A faint darkening of colour accentuated the slant of his chiselled cheekbones, his tawny eyes flaring with momentary disconcertion.

She loosed a sudden laugh, sharp in its lack of humour. 'But then why shouldn't you be?'

'What's that supposed to mean?'

'I think it means that you should get me out of this car before I say something we both regret,' Daisy admitted tightly, feeling all the volatile emotions she had buried so long ago rising up inside her without warning.

Alessio slung her a knowing look redolent of a male who knew women and prided himself on the fact. 'You never forget your first love.'

'Or what a bastard he was...' The assurance was out before Daisy could stop it.

Alessio's long, lithe frame tensed—a reaction which gave her a quite extraordinary surge of satisfaction. Shimmering eyes lanced into her with stark incredulity. 'How can you say that to me?'

'Because being married to you was the worst experience of my life,' Daisy informed him, throwing her head high.

'I beg your pardon?'

'And, believe me, I didn't require a financial bribe to persuade me into a quick exit! You were domineering, selfish and completely insensitive to what I was going through,' Daisy condemned in a shaking voice that steadily crept up in volume in spite of her attempt to control it. 'You left me at the mercy of your totally monstrous family and allowed them to treat me like dirt!

You stopped talking to me but that did not stop you *using* my body whenever you felt like it!'

Alessio was transfixed. There was no other word for his reaction. The Daisy he had married would never have criticised him. In those days, Daisy had crept around being quiet and apologetic while silently, miserably adoring him, no matter what treatment he handed out. Alessio had accepted the adoration as his right. She hadn't had the guts to stand up to him then, not when she had mistakenly blamed herself for the fact that he had *had* to marry her.

'In fact you went into a three-month-long sulk the same day that you married me! And the minute your obnoxious family saw how you were behaving they all jumped on the same bandwagon. I didn't just have one person making my life a living hell, I had a whole crowd!' she spelt out fiercely. 'And I don't care how any of you felt; I was only seventeen and I was pregnant and I did not deserve that kind of punishment!'

Daisy fell silent then. She was shattered, genuinely shattered by the bitterness that had surged up in her and overflowed. Until now she had not appreciated how deep her bitterness ran. But then she had not had an opportunity to vent those feelings before. Within forty-eight hours of her miscarriage, Vittorio Leopardi had presented her with divorce papers. And, sick to the heart from all that she had already undergone and Alessio's cruel indifference, she had signed without a word of argument.

'So, when you took the money and ran, you thought it was your due,' Alessio opined grittily.

She stole a dazed glance at him from beneath her feathery lashes. His darkly handsome features were fiercely taut. 'I ran but I didn't take any money,' she muttered wearily, and then wondered why she was still bothering to defend herself. When it came to a choice between her word and his father's, she had no doubt about whose Alessio would believe. And it wouldn't be hers.

'I despised you for what you did,' Alessio admitted with driven emphasis. 'And to listen now to you abusing my family makes me very angry.'

'I doubt if I'll lose any sleep over that.' Yet Daisy's heartbeat suffered a lurch when she met that anger brightening his hard gaze. Her chin came up, defying the sudden chill of her flesh. She had said her piece. She had waited thirteen years to say it and there wasn't a single word of it which she could honestly have taken back. How could he still behave as if he had been the only one wronged?

When she had discovered that her miscarriage had not been quite what it had appeared, she hadn't dreamt of bothering Alessio or his family with what would have been very bad news in their opinion. Indeed, still loving Alessio as she had, she had felt positively heroic protecting him from such an unwelcome announcement. He had wanted neither her nor their child, so she had taken care of the problem. She had kept her mouth shut, let the divorce proceed without interruption and brought her baby into the world alone. Alessio *owed her*! He had been able to get on with his life again, unhampered by all the many adult responsibilities that had become hers at far too young an age.

The limousine had stopped. She hadn't noticed. She gazed out at the elegant Georgian square and simply knew that she could not bear another single minute in Alessio's company. There was too much pain and confusion biting at her.

'I'm going to catch a cab back to the office and say you cancelled,' Daisy told him abruptly. 'Then you can come back on Monday if you like and see the house with someone else.'

'I don't think your boss would swallow that story.' Alessio's shrewd gaze lingered on her and his expressive mouth took on a curious quirk.

'I don't care!' Daisy stared back at him defiantly.

'So you *still* make stupid decisions on the spur of the moment.'

Colour ran up in a hot, betraying flush beneath her fine skin. She knew exactly what he was getting at. 'Shut up!' she hissed back.

'And you still blush like a furnace around me... in spite of your advanced years,' Alessio chided with lazy enjoyment at her embarrassment. 'And, in spite of *my* advanced years, you still turn me on hard and fast. Now isn't that fascinating?'

Daisy couldn't believe he had said that. The tip of her tongue stole out in a swift flick to moisten her lower lip. Involuntarily she connected with eyes that now blazed passionate gold, his ebony lashes low on his lingering scrutiny. The heavy silence stretched like a rubber band pulled too taut for safety.

'If this is your idea of a joke...' she began unevenly.

Alessio surveyed her with slumbrous intensity and a slow, devastating smile curved his mouth. 'Don't be pious. You're feeling the same thing I'm feeling right now.'

Her breath was trapped in her throat. Daisy could not tear her bemused eyes from the potent lure of his. And it was not an unfamiliar sensation that was creeping over her, she registered in dizzy disbelief; it was an old but never forgotten sensation of quite incredible excitement.

The whole atmosphere had a wild, electric charge. Her heartbeat was thundering in her eardrums, her whole body stretched and tight with every nerve-ending ready to leap.

'Curiosity and excitement,' Alessio enumerated with purring softness.

It was fatal to be so easily read but Daisy couldn't help herself. Slowly but surely she was sinking back to the level of maturity she had reached at the time of the party at which they had first met, and she remembered the sheer, terrifying *whoosh* of emotion and response which Alessio had evoked in her even at a distance of twenty feet. One look and she had been trembling, pitched on such a high of breathless, desperate yearning that she had felt slaughtered when he'd looked away again. 'Stop it...' she muttered shakily.

'I can't. I like to live dangerously now and again,' Alessio revealed huskily.

'I don't...' But her wretched body was not so scrupulous. She was devastated to feel her breasts, now full and heavy, surge against the lace barrier of her bra, the swollen nipples tightening into shameless, aching peaks.

'How would you feel about an afternoon of immoral, erotic rediscovery?' Alessio murmured thickly, his scorching golden eyes, as hot as flames, dancing over her heated skin. 'I'll take you to a hotel. For a few stolen hours, we leave the anger and the bitterness behind and relive the passion...'

Daisy was stunned, and on another level she was recalling the end of that long-ago party when Alessio had finally deigned to speak to her and make the smoothest pass she had ever encountered. She had been stunned then too by his sheer nerve. His brazen disregard of what she had naïvely seen as normal courting rituals had shocked her rigid. He had planted a drink in her hand and asked her to go to bed with him that night. She had slapped his face.

He had grinned. 'Tomorrow night?' he had asked with unconcealed amusement in his beautiful eyes, and she should have known then that it would take more than one slap to dent that ego.

'Daisy...' Alessio breathed.

This time she came back to the present with a sense of intense pain. Her violent eyes were starkly vulnerable; she veiled them. All of a sudden she felt horribly cold and lost. 'I don't want to relive the passion,' she told him tightly. 'Yes, you were quite incredible in bed but I wouldn't let you use me like that again. Once was enough. You're trying to put me down this time too. That's one advantage of being a grown-up: I can see the writing on the wall.'

The endless silence pulsed with fierce undertones.

'I *cannot* believe I am even having this conversation with you!' Alessio gritted with ferocious abruptness.

'I suppose it's comforting to know that you haven't changed. You're still a two-timing, oversexed, immoral rat,' Daisy muttered in a choky little voice, valiantly fighting off the threat of the tears damming up behind her burning eyes, ready to spill over.

'I am none of those things!' Alessio blistered back at her.

'Creep,' Daisy spat, making a dive to get out of the car. 'You really are one lousy creep to do this to me! Do you think I'm a whore or something? Do you think I don't know you're trying to humiliate me?'

A strong hand suddenly whipped out to capture one of hers, holding her back. 'It was an unfortunate impulse. I don't know what came over me. Call it temporary insanity if you like,' he growled savagely. 'I'm sorry!'

'Let go of me!'

He did, and Daisy wrenched open the door and almost fell out onto the pavement, sucking in a great gulp of fresh air as she did so. She was shaking like a leaf. She took a tottering step away from the limousine, her gait that of someone who had escaped a traumatic brush with death.

'And it's really pathetic to still be shooting the same lines at your age!' she slung back at him for good measure.

'*Dio*...will you keep your voice down?' Alessio roared at her, causing an elderly lady walking an apricot poodle to step off the pavement with a frown of well-bred disapproval and give the two of them a very wide berth.

Daisy stole a glance at Alessio, took in the shaken look of uncertainty currently clouding his normally sharp-as-paint gaze and grew in stature with the knowledge that he was handling their unexpected encounter no better than she was. Memories from their volatile teenage years and the effects of shock were driving a horse and cart through any effort they made to behave like civilised, intelligent adults.

'Look, do you want to see this house or don't you?' she asked stiffly.

'If you will control your tongue and stop hurling insults, I see no reason why we should not deal with this on a normal business footing,' Alessio drawled with icy control.

CHAPTER TWO

AN HOUR and a half later, Daisy surveyed the elegant hall of the Georgian house for the hundredth time and wondered how much more time the owners would spend entertaining Alessio. Her presence had not been required to give the grand tour, oh, dear, no!

The Raschids had stayed in specially when they had learnt that Alessio Leopardi was coming to view their beautiful home. Mr Raschid was a diplomat and apparently had met Alessio at an embassy dinner last year. Eager to renew that acquaintance, the couple had lost no time in telling Daisy to wait in the hall, while assuring Alessio that they would give him a far more interesting tour than she could. Well, she *would* have been rather out of her depth in a three-way conversation taking place in Arabic.

Alessio hadn't looked at her again. Suddenly she had acquired all the invisibility of a lowly maid. And that was how it should be. Like the Raschids, he was a client, just another client, and clients, particularly very wealthy ones, frequently treated the agency staff as something slightly less than human. When she thought about it, their romance thirteen years ago had broken all the class and status rules—Alessio the adored only son of the Leopardi banking dynasty and Daisy the au pair working down the road from his family's palatial summer villa.

They had not one single thing in common. Alessio had grown up as part of a close-knit, supportive family circle but Daisy had lost both her parents by the time she was six. Her elderly grandparents had brought her up. Her entire childhood had been filled with loss and death and sudden change. She had never had security. Illness and old age had taken everyone she cared about until her mother's sister had taken her turn of guardianship when Daisy was sixteen. A career teacher in her late thirties, Janet had encouraged her niece to be more independent than her own parents had allowed. But she had been dubious when Daisy had initially suggested spending the summer before her final year at school working as an au pair.

'I bet you land a ghastly family who treat you like a skivvy and expect you to slave for them day and night,' Janet had forecast worriedly.

In fact, Daisy had been very lucky. The agency had matched her up with a friendly, easygoing couple who owned a small villa in Tuscany and went there every summer with their children. The Morgans had given her plenty of time off and Liz Morgan had gone out of her way to see that Daisy met other young people. The very first week, Daisy had been invited to the party where she'd met Alessio.

He had roared up on a monster motorbike, sheathed in black jeans with a hole in one knee and a white T-shirt. Tousled, curly ebony hair had been blown back from his lean, vibrantly handsome features and an entire room of adolescent girls had gone weak at the knees with a collective gasp. What was more, his own sex had clustered round him with equal enthusiasm. Alessio had been hugely popular, the indisputable leader of the pack.

Even then he'd had an undeniable golden aura. One had had the feeling that even on a rainy day the sun would still shine exclusively around Alessio. He'd had the immense and boundless self-assurance of a being who

had always led a charmed life. The angels had not been
having forty winks when Alessio was born. Alessio had
been young, beautiful, academically brilliant and rich.
And Daisy's greatest attraction could only have been that
she was different from the girls he was used to dating.
The new face, the foreigner, who had to work to get a
taste of the sun, had stood out from the familiar crowd.

But she hadn't known who he was then. His name had
meant nothing to her. And even after being slapped
Alessio had still trailed her all the way back to the
Morgan villa on his motorbike when she had walked out
on the party. Since losing face in public was every teenager's worst nightmare, she had been upset. The more
she had told him to grow up and get lost, the more he
had laughed. She had been convinced that he was sending
her up for her shocked response to that proposition of
his, embarrassingly aware that she had overreacted and
that a smart verbal rejoinder would have been infinitely
more adult.

'Anyone will give me a reference. I'm a really wonderful guy when you get to know me,' he told her, with
a shimmering, teasing smile that made her vulnerable
heart sing. 'And I'm delighted you're not the sort of girl
who gives her all on a first date. Not that I would have
said no, you understand... but the occasional negative
response is probably better for my character.'

'You really like yourself, don't you?' she snapped.

'At least I don't lurk behind the furniture, scared to
speak to people, and react like a startled rabbit when
they speak to me,' he retorted, quick as a flash.

And she fled indoors, slunk up to her bedroom and
cried herself to sleep. But Alessio showed up again early
the next morning. Liz brought him into the kitchen where
Daisy was clearing up the breakfast dishes. The whole

time Alessio was with her the older woman hovered, staring at Alessio as if she couldn't quite believe he was real.

'I'll pick you up at seven...OK?' he said levelly, quite unconcerned by his audience. 'We'll go for a meal somewhere.'

'OK...'

'Smile,' he said, cheerfully ruffling the hair of the two-year-old girl clinging to his leg. 'She can smile at me...why can't you?'

'I wasn't expecting you.'

His mouth quirked. 'You're not supposed to admit things like that.'

Liz cornered her the instant he departed. 'Daisy, if I acted a little weird, put it down to me being shocked at the sight of a Leopardi entering my humble home.'

'Why?' Daisy frowned.

'We've been coming here every summer for ten years and I still can't get as much as nod of acknowledgement from the Leopardis! His parents are mega-rich—as well as their villa here they've got a huge mansion in Rome, where they live most of the time—and they are very exclusive in their friendships,' she explained uncomfortably. 'And Alessio has a reputation with girls that would turn any mother's hair white overnight. But he usually sticks with his own set. Please don't take this the wrong way, Daisy...but do you really think you can handle a young man like that? He's seen a lot more of life than you have.'

But Daisy didn't listen. Alessio did not seem remotely snobbish. And Alessio's unknown parents interested her not at all.

He rolled up in a low-slung scarlet sports car to take her out that evening. Daisy was impressed to death but

Liz grabbed her husband in horror as she peered out from behind the curtains. 'I don't believe it! They've bought a *teenager* a Ferrari! Are the Leopardis out of their minds?'

All the trappings of fantasy were there—the gorgeous guy who had miraculously picked her out of a wealth of beautiful, far more sophisticated girls, the fabulous car. That night they dined in a ritzy restaurant in Florence. Daisy was overpowered by her surroundings until Alessio reached across the table and twined her tense fingers soothingly in his, and then she quite happily surrendered to being overpowered by him instead.

On the drive back, he stopped the car, drew her confidently into his arms and kissed her. About ten seconds into that wildly exciting experience, he started teaching her *how* to kiss, laughing when she got embarrassed, laughing even harder when she tried to excuse her inexpert technique by pleading cultural differences. But surprisingly he didn't attempt to do anything more than kiss her. He was *so* different away from his friends. Romantic, tender, unexpectedly serious.

'Do you know I still haven't asked you what you're studying at college?' Alessio remarked carelessly at one point.

'History and English. I want to be an infant teacher,' she said shyly, and if he hadn't kissed her again she might have told him that she was already worrying that in a year's time she mightn't get good enough grades to make it onto the particular teacher-training course which her aunt had advised her to set her sights on.

'You wouldn't believe how relieved I am to hear that you're studying for your degree,' Alessio confided lazily. 'I was afraid you might still be at school.'

And she realised then that there had been a misunderstanding. She attended a sixth-form college for sixteen- to eighteen-year-olds, *not* a college of further education which would equip her with a degree. 'Would it have made a difference...if I had been?' she prompted uneasily.

'Of course it would have made a difference.' Alessio frowned down at her in surprise. 'I don't date schoolgirls. It may be only a matter of a couple of years but there's a huge gap in experience and maturity. You can't have an equal relationship on those terms. It would make me feel as if I had too much of an advantage and I wouldn't feel comfortable with that.'

And Daisy felt even less comfortable listening to him. She realised that Alessio would never have asked her out had he known what age she was. And that if she told him he had been given the wrong information he wouldn't want to see her again. So how could she admit to being only seventeen?

Choosing not to tell him the truth didn't feel like lying that night. It felt like a harmless pretence. She had not thought through what she was doing in allowing Alessio to believe that she was older than she was. It did not once cross her dizzy brain that there would come a time of reckoning and exposure...and that Alessio would be understandably outraged by her deception. By the end of that evening, she was walking on air and fathoms deep in love...

Daisy emerged from that unsettling recollection to find herself *still* taking up space in the Raschids' spacious hall. The sound of voices alerted her to the fact that she was about to have company again. She stood up just as the Raschids and Alessio appeared at the head of the staircase. Her uneasy eyes slid over him and lowered, but not before she'd seen his frown of surprise.

'I assumed you would have returned to the agency,' he admitted on the pavement outside.

'My boss definitely wouldn't have liked that. Have you any queries?' Daisy prompted stiffly, ignoring the chauffeur, who had the door of the limousine open in readiness.

'Yes... were you sitting in that hall the entire time I was looking round the house?'

'No, I was swinging off the chandelier for light amusement! What do you think I was doing?'

'If I had known you were waiting, I wouldn't have spent so much time with the Raschids. Did you even get a cup of coffee?'

Daisy's head was pounding. She was at the end of her rope. 'Are you trying to tell me that you care?' she derided. 'One minute you're calling me a—*Alessio!*' she gasped incredulously as he dropped two determined hands to her tiny waist, swept her very efficiently off her feet and deposited her at supersonic speed in the limousine. 'Why the heck did you do that?' she demanded breathlessly as he swung in beside her.

'If we're about to have another argument, I prefer to stage it in privacy,' Alessio imparted drily. In the time he had been away from her, he had reinstated the kind of steely control that mocked her own turbulent confusion.

'Look, I don't want another argument. I only want to go home.'

'I'll take you there.'

Daisy froze. 'No, thanks.'

'Then I'll drop you back at the agency. It's on my route.'

'You're being all polite now,' she muttered, and it infuriated her that she sounded childish.

'We both overreacted earlier.' Shrewd, dauntingly dispassionate eyes rested on her hot cheeks. 'I'm prepared to admit that I threw the first stone. Calling you a greedy bitch for accepting a settlement on our divorce was inexcusable. You were entitled to that settlement. Unfortunately, after a very few minutes in your company, I regressed to being nineteen again. But I can't see why it has to continue like that. Thirteen years is a *very* long time.'

So why all of a sudden did it feel like the fast blink of an eyelid to her? Yet she had only to look at Alessio to know how much time had passed. He no longer smouldered like a volatile volcano. Alessio now had the ability to turn freezingly cool and civil. She moistened her dry lips. 'If you're interested in the house, you won't have to deal with me again. I was standing in for someone else today.'

'And you're not a great saleswoman around me.'

'I don't even know what kind of property you're looking for.'

'You didn't ask.'

'Not much point in asking now.' Daisy sat on the edge of the seat in the corner furthest away from him.

An uncomfortable silence followed.

'I wasn't lying when I said that I still find you attractive,' Alessio breathed grimly.

Daisy tensed, her head high, her neck aching with the stress of the position.

'Nor was I trying to put you down,' Alessio drawled with an audible edge of distaste. 'But some lustful urges are better suppressed.'

A lustful urge? In her mind's eye, she pictured a sleek wolf circling a dumb sheep. And with shrinking reluctance she recalled her own response to Alessio's sexual taunting in the car earlier. Thinking about that response devastated her. For a few terrifying seconds Alessio had somehow made her want him again. And, worst of all, Alessio *knew* what he had achieved. He had resurrected an intense sexual awareness that was stronger than anything she had ever expected to feel again and she hated him for doing that—hated him for forcing her to accept that he could still have that power over her.

But then mightn't her own wanton excitement have been an echo from the past? she reasoned frantically with herself. But yes, Alessio was right on one count— you never forgot your first love, most especially not when the relationship had ended in raw pain and disillusionment.

'I think it's wise that we don't see each other again,' Alessio said quietly. 'I have to admit that I was curious but my curiosity is now satisfied.'

A painful tide of heat climbed slowly up Daisy's slender throat. Dear heaven, he was actually warning her off! Concerned lest that confession of animal lust should have roused fresh expectations in her greedy, gold-digging little heart, he was smoothly striving to kill off any ambitious ideas she might be developing. So cold, so controlled, so unapologetically superior... Her teeth gritted. How *could* Alessio talk to her like this? Did he think he was irresistible? Did he fondly imagine that she was likely to chase after him and make a nuisance of herself?

'I wasn't even curious to begin with,' she lied.

'Naturally I was curious. The last time I saw you before today you were five months pregnant and still my wife.'

Her facial muscles locked hard. 'You didn't want a wife.'

'No, I have to confess that I didn't. I doubt if you will find many teenage boys who *do* want to get married,' Alessio responded grimly. 'I was no more prepared for that commitment than you were...but I did attempt to deal with the situation—'

'Yes, you were a real hero, weren't you?' Daisy broke in with a curling lip. 'You did the honourable thing. You *married* me! Your *mamma* wept and your *papà* overflowed with sympathy. Naturally no decent Italian girl would ever have got herself in such a condition!'

'They were upset!' Alessio growled.

'Do you think *I* wasn't upset? What do you think it was like for me, being treated like some brassy little slut who had set out to trap you?' Daisy condemned painfully. 'I wasn't allowed out the door in case someone saw me! I used to have nightmares about giving birth and then being buried alive in the garden!'

'Don't be ridiculous!' Alessio gritted fiercely.

'You mean your mother didn't share that little fantasy with you? She was hoping like hell that I would have the baby and then magically disappear, leaving the baby behind! She was always telling me that I was too young to cope with a child and how much *she* loved children...' Daisy shuddered. 'Talk about feeling threatened! Life with the Leopardis...it was like a Hammer horror movie!'

Scorching eyes landed on her in near-physical assault. 'You are making me very angry.'

Daisy shrugged and compressed her generous mouth. 'That's how I remember you—*angry*. No such thing as forgiveness from a Leopardi.'

'In the circumstances, I think I behaved reasonably well.'

Daisy treated him to a glance of naked contempt. 'By making the immense sacrifice of marrying me? Don't kid yourself, Alessio. You'd have done me a bigger favour had you dumped me and run the minute I told you I might be pregnant!'

'What the hell do you have to be so bitter about?' Alessio ground out, raking her with fiercely intent eyes. *You* walked out on *me*! And anyone listening to you would think it only happened last week!'

Daisy tried and failed to swallow. For an instant her confusion and dismay were openly etched on her fragile features and then she turned her head away and saw the familiar frontage of the estate agency with a sense of incredible relief. 'Being civilised isn't easy, is it?' she conceded tightly.

'I did love you,' Alessio murmured, his intonation harsh.

As the passenger door beside her swung open, Daisy spun back to him, violet eyes bright with incredulous scorn. 'Do you think I either want or need your lies *now*?'

'Don't let me keep you,' Alessio drawled with heavy irony, shooting her a chilling look of antipathy.

The agency was closed. Of course it was. It was after one. Daisy kept on walking, tight and sick inside. This was the very worst day of her life, absolutely the very worst... seeing Alessio again, all those tearing, miserable memories fighting their way up to the surface of her mind and driving her crazy. Mere minutes away from him, she found that she couldn't believe some of the things she had said to him. No wonder he had asked her why she was so hostile! Thirteen years on and still ranting as if the divorce had only become final yesterday!

Not that Alessio had reacted much better at first. But Alessio had got a grip on himself fast. Alessio had stayed in control. Scarcely a surprise, she allowed grudgingly. Alessio had prided himself on never losing control of his temper. For the entire three and a half months of their marriage he had therefore smouldered in a silence that was infinitely more accusing and threatening and debilitating than any mere loss of temper. He had held in all his emotions with rigid, terrifying discipline at a time when Daisy had been desperate for any shred of comfort, any hint of understanding, any crumb of forgiveness. And maybe that was why in the end she had grown to hate her memory of him...

He had reduced her to the level of a tearful, pathetic supplicant, utterly destroying her pride and self-esteem. She had never had a great deal of confidence, but by the time Alessio had finished with her she had had none at all. And yet before their marriage, before everything had gone wrong, Alessio had done wonders for her confidence. He had built her up, told her off for undervaluing herself, frowned every time she cracked a joke at her own expense. He had kept on telling her how beautiful she was, how special, how happy she made *him* feel. Was it surprising that she had fallen so deeply in love with him? Or that when cruel reality had come in the door and plunged them into a shotgun marriage their whole relationship had fallen apart?

A fantastic boyfriend, a lousy husband. He had married her purely for the sake of the baby she'd been carrying. But the minute the wedding had taken place the baby had become a taboo subject. He had never mentioned her condition if he could avoid it. It had been as if he was trying to pretend she wasn't pregnant. And then one night, when the curve of her stomach had become too pronounced for him to ignore, he had abruptly turned away from her, and for those final, wretched weeks he had moved into another bedroom. The ultimate rejection…he had severed even the tenuous bond of sex.

Within days, Bianca, his twin, had been smirking at her like the wicked witch. 'Fat is a total turn-off for Alessio. Only four months along and already you look like a dumpy little barrel on short legs. He wouldn't be seen dead with you in public. Now he doesn't want to sleep with you either. Can you blame him?'

No blow had been too low for Bianca. Daisy shivered in remembrance. That spiteful tongue had been a constant thorn in her flesh. Brother and sister had been very close. She had often pictured Alessio confiding in Bianca and had cringed at the suspicion that nothing that happened in their marriage was private. She had imagined Alessio describing her as a dumpy little barrel and had wept anguished tears in her lonely bed. Strange that it had occurred to none of them that the sudden increase in her girth was not solely the result of comfort eating but a sign that she was carrying two babies and not one…

Janet's house was only round the corner from her flat. Daisy headed for her aunt like a homing pigeon, praying that Tara was still at her friend's house, wondering if some sixth sense this morning had prompted her to give in to her daughter's pleas for a little more freedom.

Janet was on the phone when she came through the back door. 'Put on the kettle,' she mouthed, and went back to her call.

Daisy took off her suit jacket, caught a glimpse of herself in the little mirror on the kitchen wall and stared in horror. She rubbed at her cheeks, bit at her lips for colour but could still only focus on the stricken look in her eyes. She hoped she hadn't looked stricken to Alessio and then questioned why it should matter to her. Pride, she supposed. Why hadn't she managed to be cool and distant? Why had she had to rave at him the way she had?

'You're quiet. Tough morning?' Janet was drawing mugs out of a cupboard.

'I bumped into Alessio today—'

A mug hit the tiled floor and smashed into about twenty pieces.

'It affected me like that too,' Daisy confided unsteadily.

'Let's go into the lounge,' her aunt suggested tautly. 'We'll be more comfortable in there.'

Daisy couldn't stay still in any case. Her nerves seemed to be leaping up and down with jumping-bean energy. She folded her arms, paced the small room and briefly outlined the bare bones of that meeting. 'And just wait until you hear this bit... His lousy father told him I *took* the money he offered me!'

Her aunt's angular face was unusually tense. 'Alessio mentioned the money?'

'He wouldn't believe me when I said that I'd refused it!'

Janet's bright blue eyes were troubled, her sallow cheeks flushed. 'Because I accepted it on your behalf.'

Daisy stopped dead in her tracks. 'You did...what?'

Her aunt walked over to her desk and withdrew a slim file from a drawer. She handed it to Daisy. 'Try to understand. You weren't thinking about the future. I was worried sick about how you would manage with a baby if anything happened to me.'

Daisy studied the older woman in a complete daze.

'It's all in the file. A financial consultant helped me to set it up. Not a penny of that money has ever been brought into this country or touched. It's in a Swiss bank account,' Janet explained. 'But it's there for you and Tara should you ever need it.'

'Alessio was telling the truth?' Daisy mumbled thickly.

Her aunt sighed. 'His father came to see me while you were in hospital. He practically begged me to accept the money. He felt terrible about the way things had turned out—'

'Like heck he did!'

Janet's face set in stern lines. 'Vittorio was sincere, Daisy. He said that you were miserable and Alessio was equally miserable and that he had felt forced to interfere—'

'He couldn't wait to interfere!'

'I found it very hard not to tell him that he *still* had a grandchild on the way,' the older woman confessed wryly. 'But, just as his loyalties ultimately lay with his son, mine lay with you. I respected your wishes.'

'But to take the money...' Daisy was shattered by that revelation.

'I still believe I made the most sensible decision. You were very young at the time. You needed financial security—'

'I've managed fine all these years without Leopardi conscience money!'

'But you mightn't have done. A lot of things could have gone wrong,' Janet pointed out. 'And what about Tara? Don't you think that she is entitled to have something from her father's family?'

'I'll give it back!' Daisy swore, too upset to listen.

'Wait and ask your daughter how she feels about that when she's eighteen. I doubt very much that Tara will feel as you feel now. She does, after all, have Leopardi blood in her veins—'

'Do you think I don't know that?' Daisy asked defensively. 'Tara knows exactly who she is—'

'No, she knows who *you* want her to be. She's insatiably curious about her father.'

Daisy was finding herself under a surprise attack from a woman she both respected and loved and it was a deeply disturbing experience. 'Since when?'

'The older she gets, the more often she mentions him. She talks about him to me. She won't ask you about him because she doesn't want to upset you.'

'I have never ducked any of her questions. I've been totally honest with her.'

Janet grimaced. 'It's going to be very difficult for you but I think it's time for you to tell Alessio that he has a daughter—'

'Are you out of your mind?' Daisy gasped, thunderstruck.

'Some day Tara is likely to march into his office in the City and announce herself...and for *her* sake Alessio ought to be forewarned.'

'I can't believe you're saying this to me.'

'Do you intend to tell Tara that you met Alessio today?'

There was a sharp little sound from behind them. Both women jerked round. Tara was standing in the hall, wide-eyed and apparently frozen to the spot by what she had overheard. Then she surged forward, her pretty face suddenly full of wild excitement. 'You met my father...Mum, you were speaking to him? Really...genuinely...speaking to him? Did you tell him about me?' she demanded, as if that revelation might have just popped out in casual conversation.

Daisy was stunned by Tara's naked excitement, by the crucifying look of hope and expectation glowing in her eyes. She was being faced with a disorientatingly different side of the daughter she had believed she knew inside out. And, shorn of the world-weary teenage front, the innocence of the child had never shone through more clearly. Icy fingers clutched at Daisy's heart. Janet had been right. Tara *was* desperate to be acknowledged by Alessio but she had carefully hidden that uncomfortable truth from her mother. Only this morning she had carelessly referred to her father as a 'major creep'.

'No... I'm afraid I didn't,' Daisy said woodenly, traumatised by what she had seen in her daughter's face.

'Your mother didn't get the opportunity,' Janet chipped in heavily.

Tara's face shuttered as if she realised how much she had betrayed and then raw resentment flared in her pain-filled eyes. 'Just because he didn't want *you* doesn't mean he mightn't want to know *me*!' she condemned with a choked sob.

Daisy went white. Her daughter stared at her in appalled silence and then took off. The kitchen door slammed on her hurtling exit.

'Lord, all I've ever done,' Daisy whispered wretchedly, 'is try to protect her from being hurt.'

'As you were?' Janet squeezed her shoulder comfortingly. 'Doesn't it ever occur to you that Alessio could ave changed as much as you have? That the teenager who couldn't cope with the prospect of fatherhood is now an adult male of thirty-two? Are you telling me that he couldn't scrape through a single meeting with Tara? That could well be enough to satisfy her and if he won't even agree to *that*...well, Tara will have to accept it. You can't protect her by avoiding the issue.'

'I guess not...' Daisy's shaken voice trailed away altogether.

Two sleepless nights had done nothing to improve Daisy's outlook on life. All she could think about as she walked into the Leopardi Merchant Bank was that in the space of one morning Alessio had brought her whole world down round her ears. And the pieces were still falling. Tara was still very upset about what she had flung at her mother in her distress. Quick-tempered and passionate, Tara was also fiercely loyal and protective. Nothing Daisy had so far said had eased her daughter's regret at having hurled those angry, hurtful words.

So why *were* you hurt? Daisy was still asking herself. There had to be something wrong with her that she could still flinch from the reminder of Alessio's rejection this long after the event. And how could she have been so blind to her daughter's very real need to know that her father had at least been made aware of her existence? Had Tara even thought of what might come next? Had she some naïve fantasy of Alessio welcoming her with open arms and delight?

Or was that her own prejudice and pessimism talking again? But Daisy could only remember Alessio's distaste when she'd been pregnant, his indifference to her need for him when she had miscarried. That had been the final bitter blow that had driven Daisy away.

Was there the remotest possibility that a male that selfish could respond in an appropriate manner to a painfully vulnerable teenage daughter whom he had never wanted in the first place? Daisy acknowledged that she *had* known what she was doing when she'd kept quiet about Tara's existence. The risk of exposing her child to the same rejection that she herself had experienced had been too great.

Daisy got out of the lift on the top floor. If she had thought Giles's office was the last word in luxury, she was now learning her mistake. The sleek smoked-glass edifice which housed the Leopardi Merchant Bank was stunningly elegant in its contemporary decor. There were two women in the reception area. The older one moved forward. 'Miss Thornton? I'm Mr Leopardi's secretary. Could you come this way, please...?'

Daisy reddened. Alessio's secretary wore a marked look of strain—possibly the result of Daisy's steadfast determination not to be refused an appointment. Alessio was undoubtedly furious. After all, he had made it very clear that he did not wish to see her again. However, she didn't know where he lived so she had had no choice but to approach him at the bank.

Her heart pounding at the foot of her throat and reverberating in her eardrums, she walked dizzily into Alessio's office, a great big room with a great big glass desk and...Alessio standing there, suppressed dark fury and rigid restraint emanating from every lean, poised line of his tall, muscular body.

'What the hell are you doing here?' he demanded with icy precision.

Her head swam, her knees wobbled. She opened her mouth and closed it again. A quite sickening wave of dizziness overwhelmed her and the next thing she knew the blackness was folding in and her legs were crumpling beneath her.

CHAPTER THREE

DAISY surfaced from her faint very slowly. She focused on Alessio's dark features as he swam gradually into focus, and a dazed smile curved her soft mouth. He was cradling her in his arms, her slight body still limp, her head resting back against his forearm. It felt wonderful. Her violet eyes dreamy, she looked up at him...and melted, a honeyed languor stealing through her as she shifted and curled her toes in wanton anticipation.

'You have the most gorgeous eyes,' Alessio breathed in an abstracted undertone, drawing ever closer.

They were lost in his. Pools of passionate gold set between luxuriant black lashes even longer than her own. Daisy expelled a tiny sigh, the raw heat of his lean, hard body curling sensuously into her relaxed limbs. She curved instinctively closer and he lifted a hand almost jerkily and let long brown fingers thread into the fall of her hair, his thumb rubbing caressingly against her earlobe. Her heartbeat went crazy in the thrumming silence.

'Alessio...' she mumbled.

'*Piccola mia...*' The familiar endearment left him in an aching sigh.

Warm fingers cupped her cheekbone as he bent his dark head. He captured her moist lips in a devouring kiss and plundered them apart. From that first instant of contact, Daisy was electrified. The erotic flick of his tongue exploring the tender interior of her mouth made her jerk in shock and gasp. Lightning heat sizzled through her. Her hands came up to clutch at his thick hair, his broad shoulders, his powerful arms and clung. Every clamouring sense roared off in glorious rediscovery. He crushed her to him and she surrendered with enthusiasm. As she strained up to him in a fever of desire, excitement clawed at her throbbing body in a voracious surge.

With a driven groan, Alessio dragged his mouth from hers and stared down at her with stunned intensity. He snatched in a ragged breath and abruptly stood up, carrying her slim body with him. His strong face set like cement as he gazed into her passion-glazed eyes. Swinging lithely round, he simply opened his arms and let her drop from a height back down onto the sofa he had just vacated.

'Give me the *bad* news first!' Alessio raked down at her.

Daisy had landed in a mess of wildly tangled hair and inelegantly splayed limbs on the mercifully well-sprung sofa. She didn't know what had hit her. For an instant she didn't even know where she was but she knew that Alessio was there all right, standing over her like a hanging judge as she attempted to halt a seemingly unstoppable roll in the direction of his plush office carpet. A pair of strong hands caught her and impatiently flipped her back upright into the corner of the seat.

' "The bad news..."?' Daisy echoed. Momentarily, utter cowardice had her in its hold. She didn't *want* to be forced to think. Not about how time had cruelly slid back to entrap and humiliate her. Not about how excruciatingly pleasurable it had felt to be in Alessio's arms. Not about how dreadful it felt to be separated from him again. No, she definitely didn't want to think.

'You only faint when you're terrified! Do you think
I don't remember that?' Alessio launched at her grimly.
'You drop in a pathetic little heap, then you open those
big blue eyes and fix them on me and I have an uncontrollable urge to give way to my baser instincts. That's
how you broke the news of your pregnancy!'

'*My* pregnancy?' Daisy questioned helplessly. 'I didn't
get that way on my own!'

'There was nothing accidental about it,' Alessio condemned harshly.

Daisy froze, shattered by that particular accusation.
Even thirteen years ago, it had not occurred to her that
Alessio might believe that her pregnancy was anything
other than an accident. That his family suspected her of
such manipulative behaviour had been no surprise to her,
but she had innocently assumed that at least Alessio did
not share their suspicions. 'Are you really trying to accuse
me of having deliberately set out to...?'

Alessio spread two brown hands in a frustrated
movement of dismissal. 'We are not going to talk about
this.'

'Now just you wait a minute,' Daisy objected,
springing upright. 'You can't throw an accusation like
that and then back off from it again!'

'Did you hear me? Leave yesterday's bad news where
it belongs,' Alessio spelt out. 'We are not about to get
into that again. We are not going to fight about ancient
history like a couple of stupid kids!'

'Ancient history...yesterday's bad news...' How would
Alessio react when she informed him that 'yesterday's
bad news' was infinitely more current than he had had
any cause to suspect? The fight went out of Daisy. She
sank heavily back down on the sofa again. 'You want

to know why I told your secretary I had to see you to discuss an urgent, confidential matter—'

'I think I'm ahead of you there.' Alessio surveyed her with innate cynicism, his lip curling. 'You're broke, aren't you? You're in debt.'

'I don't know where you get that idea.' But Daisy turned a guilty pink, unable to avoid thinking about that Swiss bank account filled with Leopardi money. Not just filled but positively *bursting* at the seams with Leopardi money, the original investment having grown greatly in the intervening years, according to Janet.

Alessio settled down on the matching leather sofa opposite. He looked incredibly formidable to her evasive eyes. He was wearing a superbly tailored navy pinstriped suit and a red silk tie. The expensive fabric skimmed wide shoulders and delineated long, powerful thighs. Hurriedly she tore her gaze from him but he stayed there in her mind's eye. So achingly handsome, from the top of his smooth, darkly beautiful head to the soles of his equally beautiful shoes. Her throat closed over. Her mind was a complete blank. Why couldn't he have started losing some of his hair or developed a bit of a businessman's paunch?

'Daisy, my time is at a premium. Since you forced this meeting by giving my secretary no opportunity to deny your demand, I had to cancel an important appointment to free a space for you—'

'A space on the sofa?' she bit out between gritted teeth.

'At this moment, I think the less said about that development the better.'

Bitter resentment tensed Daisy. Alessio... all heat and passion one moment, polar ice the next. Daisy had never had his trick of switching off, had never been able to understand how he could make mad, passionate love to her in the night and then turn away from her when she tried to talk. When her emotions were involved, she wore everything on the surface, could not hold her feelings back. But Alessio locked everything away and kept a ferociously tight hold on the key.

'To be frank, I'm not surprised that you have financial problems,' Alessio imparted coolly. 'I imagine the divorce settlement went a long time ago—'

'And why do you imagine that?'

'At that age you would have had no idea how to handle that amount of money. But I'm relieved that you are finally acknowledging that you did receive that settlement,' he drawled. 'It was very naïve of you to assume that I wouldn't know about it and that you could afford to lie.'

'I wasn't lying.'

'Being inventive with the truth...*again*?' Alessio asked very drily.

Daisy went pale and involuntarily glanced up, connecting with brilliant eyes alive with derision. 'I only ever told you one lie...*only* one. I let you think I was at university when I wasn't. You never actually asked me what age I was—'

'Semantics,' Alessio dismissed, unimpressed and not one whit more yielding or forgiving on the point than he had been in the past. 'I also thought we had reached an agreement, Daisy. The past is off limits. Let's strive to keep the temperature down. Perhaps I should speed up matters by admitting that because we were once married I do still feel some sense of responsibility towards you.'

Daisy stiffened and bridled. 'I don't want you feeling responsible for me and I am not here to ask you for a loan. But, while we're on the subject, let me assure you that I would die of starvation before I would ask you for help!'

'Then exactly what *are* you doing here?' Alessio enquired.

Daisy breathed in deep and dug into her slim handbag to extract a copy of Tara's birth certificate and a small photograph. Her slender hands were trembling, her stomach knotting up. She gripped the certificate. 'This is going to come as a big shock to you, Alessio... but I'm afraid that there isn't any easy way to do this—'

'Do what?' he broke in impatiently.

Daisy stood up on wobbly legs, her heart thumping as if she were tied to the rails in front of an express train. 'I think I'll just leave these with you and then maybe I could ring you tomorrow and see how you feel.'

Alessio had already vaulted upright. His dark features were taut. 'What the hell are you talking about?'

'After we split up, I discovered that I had been expecting twins... and although I had lost o-one of them,' Daisy stammered, a trickle of nervous perspiration running down between her breasts below her blouse, 'I didn't lose the other.'

Alessio stared down at her with fiercely narrowed eyes, a stark frown of bewilderment drawing his level black brows together. 'What are you trying to say?'

'I have a daughter of thirteen... *your* daughter,' she delivered with unconscious stress as she took an automatic step back from him.

'That's impossible.' The faintest tremor lent an uneven quality to Alessio's usually level diction and his accent had thickened. 'You had a miscarriage.'

'She was born three months after I left Italy. I was kept in hospital right up until her birth... in case I lost her too. She was a couple of weeks premature. You see,

I wasn't quite as pregnant as everyone assumed I was,' Daisy muttered awkwardly in the thundering silence of Alessio's total disbelief. 'The doctor in Rome got the delivery date wrong because when he first saw me I was bigger than he thought I should be, but that was because I was carrying twins.'

'You had a miscarriage,' Alessio delivered in stubborn repetition. 'And if at some subsequent stage you did give birth to a baby which was premature it could not possibly have been mine—'

'Tara was born in April.' Daisy's lips compressed tremulously.

If Alessio had been capable of rational thought, his intelligence would have told him that given the time period concerned there was no way on earth that the child could be anything other than his. But then Alessio was not reasoning out anything right now. Alessio was at a standstill, blocked from moving on by the barrier of what he had believed to be concrete fact for thirteen years.

'You lost the baby,' he said, his rich drawl oddly attentuated and unevenly pitched.

Daisy couldn't stop staring at him. His strong bone structure was fiercely prominent below his golden skin. He was alarmingly pale. His astute eyes were curiously dark and unfocused.

'I didn't lose Tara... I lost her twin,' Daisy whispered shakily, her eyes aching. 'But when I left Rome I didn't know that. What I did know was that you didn't want me or the baby, and once the baby was no longer on the way there was no reason for us to stay married. You couldn't wait to get rid of me. You couldn't even bring yourself to come and commiserate at the hospital because naturally you couldn't help being relieved that it was all over—'

'*Madre di Dio...*' Alessio breathed unsteadily, his lean hands suddenly clenching into powerful fists.

'And I don't blame you for that...not really,' Daisy admitted with innate honesty, her voice taut with the force of her own turbulent emotions. 'But I had had enough and the last thing I could have faced was breaking back into all your lives when you thought you were finally free of me and saying, Guess what? I'm *still* pregnant! It was easier to let you go on thinking that that was over, finished and done with, the way you all wanted it to be. So I really didn't want to have to come here this morning and spoil your day—'

'Spoil my day?' Alessio enunciated with visible difficulty.

Daisy stooped almost clumsily and dropped the certificate and the small photo on the low glass table between them. 'I would never have told you if it had been left solely up to me,' she revealed in a jerky undertone as she began backing away towards the door, her anxious violet gaze nailed to his low shimmering golden eyes. 'I know you're shocked and angry and undoubtedly thinking that you must have been cursed the night you first met me but please try to think of all this from Tara's point of view. She would like to meet you. She's not going to make a nuisance of herself or anything like that but she's curious—'

'Where the bloody hell do you think you're going?' In a sudden movement, Alessio sprang out of his statue-like stillness and strode after her.

'I've said all I've got to say for now!' Daisy confessed, and speeded up in her path to the door, wrenching it open when she got there and not bothering to look over her shoulder as she walked very fast down the corridor. She hit the call button on the lift and then looked.

'*Dio!* Get back here right now!' Alessio launched at her in a rage, from a distance of twenty feet.

Her heart leapt into her throat. She had a dazed impression of the receptionist's stunned incredulity and then she turned and fled, heading for the stairs instead. There was no point in assisting Alessio to spring an embarrassing scene in public. Obviously he was in deep shock, otherwise he wouldn't have shouted at her like that. He was also in a blaze of fury, and that was new—but not something Daisy planned to hang around and find out more about. She crashed through the last set of fire doors and raced down a wide set of stairs.

'I'll drag you up again by the hair if you don't get back here!' Alessio roared down at her from the flight above.

'I'm running away for your benefit, not my own!' Daisy hurled breathlessly back. 'If I don't, you'll say a lot of things that you'll be deeply ashamed of saying in a few hours' time!'

'You bitch!' Alessio grated as he continued his enraged pursuit.

'Don't you dare call me that!' Daisy paused to shout back. 'And by the way, it was *your* birth control that failed and not my *lack* of it! The dates prove that beyond doubt!'

Alessio spat something in Italian that sounded very aggressive. Daisy blenched. This was not a mood she knew him in—Alessio in an uncontrollable dark fury, doubtless made all the more dangerous by his lack of practice in expressing such feelings. It had not once crossed her mind that she might find herself being chased through the Leopardi Merchant Bank by a male who even at nineteen had prided himself on his self-control and superhuman cool. So he was furious—well, that was no surprise, was it? But that was no excuse to attack her!

Tara had been conceived in August, not July, which meant that Alessio was the one responsible. Of course, he had tried to push that responsibility off onto her, citing the very first time they had made love, when a slight misunderstanding had occurred and he had falsely assumed that she was protected from pregnancy. Even with Alessio in hot pursuit, Daisy was childishly delighted to have finally been able to throw that important fact in his teeth.

'Watch out! You're going to fall and break your neck!' Alessio blazed, sounding far too close for comfort.

In her attempt to speed up, Daisy missed her footing and lurched forward. She gasped as a powerful hand suddenly closed on the collar of her jacket to steady her and haul her back up a safe step. Whisking her round, Alessio imprisoned her between his hard, muscular length and the landing wall without noticing that her feet were no longer connected to solid ground.

'*Dio*...how dare you accuse me of being relieved when you lost our baby?' Alessio thundered down at her, glittering golden eyes splintering with violent anger, his hands anchored to her narrow ribcage to hold her entrapped. 'I went on a binge! I got so damned drunk, I nearly killed myself! I didn't have the guts to come to that hospital...I was too *ashamed* to face you! I didn't know what to say when it was too late to say it. "Sorry" wasn't likely to cover it when our baby was dead!'

As he slowly released her, she slid down the wall again and one of her shoes fell off but Daisy wasn't up to fumbling blindly for it. Keeping herself balanced on tiptoe on one side, she gaped up at him, violet eyes wide with astonishment at what he was telling her.

'I showed up three days later and you had gone,' Alessio added unsteadily, dense dark lashes screening his gaze from her, but not before she had seen the savage pain and guilt in the stormy depths of his darkened eyes. 'My father told me that if I put one foot onto a flight for London he would personally kill me! He said I'd done enough damage. But I didn't listen to him until Bianca told me about the money and convinced me that that was all you had wanted from the start—'

'I doubt you needed much persuasion.'

'You'd gone,' Alessio said again. 'You agreed to a divorce without even discussing it with me!'

'But that's what you wanted,' Daisy pointed out very shakily.

Aggressively taut, his strong face shuttered, Alessio took a step back from her. Her throat was working, her insides churning, but all she could think about was the fierce pain and remorse he had revealed—feelings that she had never once dreamt he might be experiencing in the aftermath of their breakup.

The noisy sound of a door swinging back on its hinges came from above them, followed by the echo of chattering female voices.

'Come back upstairs,' Alessio demanded harshly.

Daisy dug her foot back into her lost shoe and sidled away from him, terrified that she was about to break down in tears in front of him. Right now, she didn't think that she could cope with any more. And she had done what she had come to do. She had told him about Tara and he needed time to think about that. Did he appreciate that himself? Was that why he had concentrated on their past rather than on the revelation that he had a daughter? Or was the reality more that he had not yet been able even to begin to absorb that news?

'I'll phone you...t-tomorrow,' Daisy stammered sickly, gripping the handrail with a perspiring palm as she immediately began to head downwards again.

Alessio ground out a frustrated imprecation in his own language as the footsteps above grew louder and closer.

Daisy took advantage of the approaching company to flee, and she didn't glance back this time. Tears were blinding her as she reached the final flight of stairs. The heel of one of her shoes went skittering off the edge of a step and she fell heavily with a bitten-off gasp of fright. Briefly her body was numbed by the force of her fall. Then the pain came in a stomach-churning surge. Slowly, painfully she breathed in deep and picked herself up, straightened her rucked skirt with a trembling hand and limped out through the doors into the ground-floor foyer.

She caught a cab back to the agency. Her hip throbbed with the bruises she had inflicted on herself. But that physical discomfort was as nothing to the terrible pain and confusion tearing at her fast-crumbling composure. Using the rear entrance from the car park, she hobbled into the stark little room that the sales team used for coffee-breaks and collapsed down on an armchair.

You're like an accident around Alessio, she told herself wearily. But then even before she had met him her life had lurched from one disaster to the next. Why had she expected anything to change? She scolded herself for thinking like that. It was a loser's mindset which she had put behind her a long time ago. But somehow, when a real crisis loomed, it was hard to forget the childhood which had left her so desperately insecure, that insidious, confidence-zapping feeling that everything that went wrong was *always* her fault.

Yet that sun-drenched summer with Alessio had, ironically, been the happiest of her life. Feeling loved and wanted and needed had been an intoxicating new experience for Daisy. They had been inseparable and at the time that intensity had seemed mutual. Of course, in actuality, she conceded painfully, she had only been one more notch on Alessio's bedpost. A naïve pushover, always available, always willing, frankly asking to be slapped in the teeth, she thought now. What little common sense she had possessed had evaporated beneath the onslaught of Alessio's first smile.

The real reason why Alessio had not dated schoolgirls should have been obvious to her even then. He had been long past the stage of settling for a goodnight kiss at the end of a date. Daisy had been smoothly, gently but quite ruthlessly seduced by a teenager already expert in the field of sexual intimacy.

Of course, he had also talked with passionate conviction about how much he loved her and how he would fly over and see her at weekends after she went home, but then he *would* have said that, wouldn't he? Such assurances were par for the course. Daisy was convinced that if she hadn't got pregnant, if she had returned to London she would never have heard from Alessio Leopardi again. After all, he had already had a steady girlfriend at university, but Sophia had been abroad that summer...

Daisy swam back to the present, feeling utterly drained. She asked herself why she had been so devastated to hear Alessio admit that he had been too ashamed and upset to face her after her miscarriage. That he had got drunk, been ripped apart by guilt and an obvious inability to cope with either her feelings or his own. She had been shattered by the realisation that her image of Alessio had been inexplicably trapped in a time-warp.

At seventeen, she had looked up to him, depended on him, viewed him as an experienced and strong adult in comparison with herself. It had not occurred to her then that Alessio might have weaknesses of his own. Only now did she think he *was* only six years older than Tara is now; beneath the glossy, cool front he was only a kid too. But Daisy had made a hero of him because nothing less than a hero could have made her feel safe in the new and threatening world in which he and his family lived.

Tears had dampened her face. Daisy pressed unsteady hands to her wet cheeks. Telling Alessio about Tara had somehow brought all those painful feelings of inadequacy back again. But that was the past and far behind her now, she reminded herself. Taking a deep breath, she stood up again and set about eradicating the evidence that she had been crying.

Her phone was ringing when she reached her desk. She swept up the receiver a split second before Barry the Barracuda reached for it. He lounged back against her desk, curious brown eyes nailed to her, a faint smirk on his handsome mouth. 'You seem a little harassed...anything wrong?'

Daisy shook her head, carefully avoiding his hotly appreciative appraisal. Even though she was as encouragingly warm as an ice sculpture around Barry, he had buckets of persistence. One minor pleasantry and Barry would be back to embarrassing the hell out of her by telling her what a good time an older woman could have with a younger man.

She put the receiver to her ear.

'Daisy?'

Her heart lurched violently against her breastbone. It was Alessio. 'What do you want?' she whispered.

'You ... *now*,' Alessio spelt out succinctly. 'I'm in the wine bar on the corner. You have five minutes to get here.'

The line went dead. Daisy straightened, deathly pale, and then reached for her bag again.

Alessio was in the darkest corner of the bar. As she walked towards him, he sprang fluidly upright and surveyed her with glittering eyes that were as hard as jet, his lean, powerful frame whip-taut with sizzling tension.

'I promised I'd ring you tomorrow,' Daisy reminded him defensively.

'I want to meet my daughter and I am not prepared to await your convenience,' Alessio gritted in a fierce undertone.

'She's at school.'

'*Where?*'

As she sat down, Daisy looked at him in appalled comprehension. 'You can't go there—'

'When does she get out?' Alessio growled.

'You're not thinking straight,' Daisy protested, shaken by the immediacy of his demand. 'Tara didn't even know I was coming to see you today.'

His eyes flared. '*Dio* ... you should be locked up! You breeze into the bank after thirteen years of silence and tell me I have a daughter! Then you walk out again and tell *me* I'm not thinking straight? What kind of a woman are you?'

A woman who had not enjoyed being forced to break the same 'bad news' twice in one lifetime, she thought.

'I still can't credit that you have done this to me,' Alessio confessed with barely suppressed savagery, driving not quite steady fingers through his luxuriant black hair and surveying her with more than a glimmering of stark incredulity. 'That you could be so bitter you would conceal the birth of my child from me—'

'I wasn't bitter then. I thought I was doing you a favour.'

'A *favour*?' Alessio queried in rampant disbelief.

A suffocating silence hummed.

'I believed you would be happier not knowing,' Daisy finally admitted.

'*Happier...?*'

'Obviously I was wrong,' Daisy conceded in a tense rush. 'I wish you would stop looking at me like that...like I belong in a lunatic asylum or something... I never had the slightest idea that you would feel like *this* about it!'

As Alessio got a grip on his seething emotions, chilling dark golden eyes closed in on her. 'It was a despicable act. Whatever mistakes I made, I did not deserve to be kept in ignorance of my daughter's existence. We were still married when she was born. Your silence was indefensible. Don't try to excuse it—'

'Maybe I could take this kind of talk better if you had once shown the slightest interest or concern for your child *before* she was born!' Daisy dared shakily, for there was something about the way Alessio was talking now which sent a compulsive shiver down her spine.

'I demonstrated my concern by marrying you. I did not once suggest any other means of dealing with our predicament. Nor, you may recall, did my family,' Alessio reminded her coldly.

'But you still didn't *want* the baby,' Daisy argued feverishly, desperate to hear him admit that fact.

Alessio sent her a look of derision. 'Why else did I marry you if not for our child's sake?'

Daisy snatched in a shaken breath, stunned by the whiplash effect of that one dauntingly simple question.

'I think I need a little time to come to terms with this *before* I meet my daughter.' Having made that charged acknowledgement from between clenched teeth of reluctance, Alessio abruptly thrust his glass away. 'Keep Tara home on Wednesday. I'll call around ten. I'll take her out somewhere. At this moment,' he asserted with icy conviction, 'I have nothing more to say to you.'

'You'll need the address.'

In the shattering, pulsing silence which followed, Daisy, employing his gold pen, scrawled her address on the back of the business card he presented to her.

Alessio stood up. 'If it is the last thing I do in this lifetime, I will punish you for this,' he swore half under his breath.

Daisy was left alone with an uncorked bottle of vintage wine and two untouched glasses. Her knees were knocking together under the table. For a weak moment, she was seriously tempted to try drowning her sorrows. Guilt and bewilderment were tearing her apart. Alessio was outraged and appalled by what she had done. And Daisy was in shock. Alessio, who had once blithely leapt in where angels feared to tread, was backing off for two days to take stock of the situation. Why did that frighten her even more?

CHAPTER FOUR

THE doorbell went in two short, impatient bursts. It was only twenty past nine.

'Do you think it's *him*?' Tara shrieked in panic from her bedroom. 'My hair's still wet!'

Daisy skimmed damp palms down her slender thighs, breathed in deep and opened the door. It was Alessio, strikingly elegant in a pearl-grey suit, pale blue silk shirt and tie.

'I thought you'd be at work.'

'I took the morning off,' Daisy told his tie.

'Does that mean you're planning to accompany us?' The ice in that rich dark drawl let her know how unwelcome an idea that was.

'No...but Tara's not ready yet. Would you like to come in?' Daisy enquired, her fingernails scoring purple crescents into her palms. His cold hostility bit deep.

'I'll wait in the car.'

Her tremulous mouth tautened. 'Alessio...please don't make this any more difficult than it already is.'

There was a sharp little silence.

He released his breath in a hiss and thrust the door shut. The fierce tension in Daisy's slight shoulders gave a little. She walked into the lounge. 'Would you like some coffee?'

He uttered a cool negative.

'She'll be a while. She's not even dressed yet. She was earlier, though. She got up at seven and trailed out her whole wardrobe. Then she decided she needed to wash her hair...' Conscious that she was babbling, Daisy compressed her lips and jerkily folded her arms. She no longer had any excuse to avoid looking at him.

Alessio's vibrantly handsome features were ferociously tense, his strong jawline harshly set. A frown drew his ebony brows together. He looked back at her with glittering golden eyes that chilled her to the marrow. 'What did I do that was so bad that you had to steal my child from me?'

Daisy's strained eyes burned and she spun away, not trusting herself to speak. An intimidating amount of bitter incomprehension had splintered through that demand.

'With that poor a start to our marriage, we were bound to have some problems,' Alessio continued harshly. 'But we had no arguments.'

Daisy almost smiled. To argue with someone you had to speak to them, didn't you? And doormats did not start arguments. Alessio had been able to stride about being mean, moody and silently macho without the smallest challenge from her corner. Indeed, Daisy had grown steadily more afraid of what she might hear if he did break that silence.

'I was never deliberately unkind to you,' Alessio asserted.

Daisy resisted an urge to mention his reconciliation with his former girlfriend, Sophia. Why dig up something so long buried? It would be demeaning and petty to confront him about that now. Teenage boys were not programmed for fidelity. And she didn't even know if he had been sleeping with the other girl or merely seeking out more entertaining company. She wanted to be fair. Their marriage had been over by then anyway.

Their relationship had really died the night when Alessio had turned away from her in bed. Thinking back to that devastating rejection, Daisy relived the anguish of a very insecure teenage girl who had been prepared to settle for sex if that was all she could have from the boy she loved. When Alessio had decided he didn't want or need the sex either, she felt utterly devalued and useless, instead of feeling relieved that so degrading a practice had ended. A couple of weeks after Alessio had moved out of their bedroom, Bianca had dropped the news about Sophia. Alessio's sister had enjoyed telling Daisy that her brother was seeing the other girl again.

'And, even though I then believed that you had chosen to become pregnant, I never once confronted you with that belief.' Alessio, Daisy registered, sounded very much as though he expected a burst of applause for such saint-like restraint.

'Why not?' she couldn't help asking.

'I assumed that you had done it so that you would not have to leave me at the end of the summer.'

Daisy reddened to the roots of her hair. She did it because she loved me...she just couldn't help herself. Trust Alessio to come up with an excuse for her that flattered him! But no wonder he had felt trapped; no wonder he had been so furiously angry with her throughout their short-lived marriage!

'And what would have been the point? Would it have changed anything? After all, I had already screwed up both our lives with spectacular efficiency,' Alessio derided, his wide, sensual mouth narrowing. 'I had failed my own expectations, bitterly disappointed and distressed my parents and got a very young girl pregnant. That was quite enough to be going on with, do you not think?'

Daisy cloaked her pained gaze. His every word tore at her and increased her confusion. It seemed inconceivable to her now, but back then she had never thought in any depth about the effect of their marriage on Alessio's relationship with his parents. Her adolescent outlook had been narrow and exclusive, centred solely on her own feelings and what was happening in *their* relationship. She had taken no account of all the other pressures on Alessio. Her belated acknowledgement of her own essential teenage selfishness dismayed her.

'And now I come here to meet a daughter who is a stranger,' Alessio breathed grimly. 'Have you any idea how that feels? A daughter whom I would have loved and cared for and protected has been living all this time within miles of the Leopardi bank in the City...and here she is in a grubby little flat you couldn't swing a cat in!'

Suddenly, Daisy wanted to cover her ears. 'I didn't think you would want her—'

'Is that what you have told her? Have you poisoned *her* mind against me as well?' Alessio dealt her a fierce look of condemnation. 'And still you do not tell me what I did to deserve such a punishment. So I wasn't *man* enough to make it to the hospital...but that was the one and only time I ever let you down!'

Daisy's knees wouldn't hold her up any more. She dropped down on the edge of an armchair. 'I'm sorry,' she mumbled thickly.

Alessio had stridden over to the window. He swung back to study her with bleak, darkened eyes, all emotion firmly back under lock and key. 'I can do without the tears. If my daughter sees them, no doubt I'll get the blame for that too, and I have no desire to make a first impression as some sort of big, nasty bully who makes her mother cry!'

Daisy gulped and scrabbled hurriedly for a tissue.

'As of now we can only look to the future and hope to do better this time around,' Alessio completed with hard, lingering emphasis, his screened eyes, with a sudden stormy flare of glinting gold, resting on her downbent silver head. 'Our daughter's needs *must* come first. We both owe her that consideration. I hope you appreciate that fact.'

Daisy was too choked up to speak. She was thinking about the pathetic little exercise book that Tara had produced from its hiding place on the top of her wardrobe. Some pictures of Alessio, carefully cut out of newspapers, had been glued into it. In her frantic excitement last night, Tara had bared her soul, hadn't been able to hold anything back. And Daisy had tossed and turned in her bed until dawn, coming to shamefaced terms with the fact that she had never offered her daughter a photograph of her father. Yet she had a thirteen-year-old photograph of Alessio still lurking in her own purse. For the first time, it struck her that that was just a tad peculiar and rather hard to explain rationally.

'Excuse me,' she said, and made a dive for the door.

When she had managed to compose herself again, she popped her head round Tara's bedroom door. 'Are you ready yet?'

Tara was sitting on the edge of the bed, unusually still. Glossy streamers of black hair rippled as she turned her head, her anxious eyes so painfully like her father's that Daisy's heart skipped a startled beat. 'I'm terrified,' she whispered jerkily. 'I've thought about this for so long, but now it's really happening, now he's actually *here* . . . suppose he doesn't like me?'

Daisy recalled Alessio's restive, simmering tension. 'He's just as scared you won't like him.'

'Is he?' Tara scrambled up, bolstered by the assurance. 'Did he say so?'

'No, but it's written all over him,' Daisy managed with a wobbly smile.

'I guess this is hard for him too. Maybe he thinks I'm expecting Superdad or something.' Tara's eyes softened, her tender heart instantly touched. 'I mean, he won't know what to do or say either. I suppose it's easier for me really... I've always known about him.'

'Yes.' Daisy watched the carpet begin to blur under her aching gaze.

'And he must be dead keen, to arrive this early,' Tara decided.

'Yes—'

'I'm being really cruel staying in here and keeping him waiting,' Tara concluded with a sudden frown of discomfiture.

Having reached the conclusion that her father was more to be pitied than she was, Tara straightened her slim shoulders and stepped round her mother. 'It's OK... you don't need to come. I think I'd prefer to see him on my own first.'

Daisy flattened herself up against the wall and wrapped her arms round herself. Alessio wouldn't want an audience either. So why should she feel excluded? Her daughter was no longer a baby who needed her every step of the way and Tara had always had a strong streak of independence.

In the lounge they both spoke at the same time.

'You look like my sister...' she heard Alessio breathe raggedly.

'Do you still have your motorbike?' Tara asked in a rather squeaky rush.

Daisy pressed her fingers against her wobbly mouth, yanked herself off the wall which had been supporting her and fled into the kitchen. Where was all this truly slaughtering guilt coming from? she asked herself wretchedly. Did she have to accept that she'd been completely in the wrong to keep father and daughter apart?

But how easy it was for Alessio to heap all the blame on her! Thirteen years ago, he had not made a single attempt to share his real feelings with her. So, naturally, Daisy had made assumptions. His behaviour had led her to believe that she was making the right decision, but why had it not occurred to her that she might only be storing up trouble for the future? Yes, it was very easy for Alessio to condemn her now. Hindsight made everyone wise. He could say now that he would have loved and cared for his daughter, and how could she challenge him when he had never been put to the test?

And what was going to happen to her relationship with her daughter if Tara started thinking the same way? Did she deserve to be treated like some sort of unfeeling monster? But how much had she been protecting *herself* from further pain and humiliation when she'd chosen not to tell Alessio about Tara? Daisy dashed a hand over her streaming eyes. And what if Alessio proved to be a terrific father? Just to spite her, just to prove her wrong and himself right, Alessio would very probably break his neck to be Superdad and, the next thing she knew, Tara would bitterly resent having been denied her father all these years.

'Mum...we're away!' Tara called from the hall.

Before Daisy could respond, the front door slammed. From the lounge window she watched Tara walking admiringly all the way round the gleaming black Maserati that Alessio had evidently arrived in. She was chattering and laughing non-stop. She looked as if someone had lit a torch inside her. Alessio was visibly entranced by that glowing volubility. His absorption in his excited daughter was total.

And why not? Daisy thought painfully. In looks and personality, Tara was very much a Leopardi. Strongwilled, stubborn, outspoken and passionate, she was Alessio without the ice and self-control, Bianca without the spite and spoilt-rich-girl arrogance. Daisy would have had to be blind not to recognise that. And how much easier it must be for Alessio to relate to that laughing, talkative girl who bore so little resemblance to her mother. A cold, hard knot of fear clenched in Daisy's stomach as she gazed down at them. Breathing in deeply, she moved away from the window.

When she got back from work, Tara still wasn't home. It was after ten that evening when the bell went. Daisy went to the door, expecting it to be Tara but wondering why she hadn't used her key. Thirty seconds later, she knew why. Her daughter came through the door, smothering a yawn, with Alessio a mere step behind her. Caught unprepared, Daisy was appalled. She stood there barefoot, clad in a pair of old jeans and a T-shirt that had shrunk in the wash, while Alessio looked as infuriatingly immaculate and sleekly beautiful as he had done twelve hours earlier.

'I've had a fantastic day,' Tara confided, engulfing her small, stiff mother in a brief hug without even noticing her tension. 'But I'm really tired. 'Night, Dad.'

Dad? She said it so naturally, so easily that Daisy was shaken. As Tara vanished into her bedroom, she met Alessio's shrewd gaze and hurriedly cloaked her own.

'I'll take that cup of coffee now,' he drawled smoothly.

Daisy's cheeks coloured. For an instant, she had a dismaying image of herself hovering like a little girl obediently awaiting her instructions and Alessio taking control of the situation in his own good time. 'Coffee,' she said tightly, and marched into the kitchen, leaving him to find his own way into the lounge.

So Tara and her father had got on like a house on fire. She was pleased for them both—she *was*! A good relationship with Alessio could only benefit her daughter. Now that Tara had met him, the ice was broken and they could all settle down into the kind of detached sharing practised by thousands of divorced parents. Alessio and Tara would form a relationship in which Daisy would play little part.

Maybe she was a bit jealous of that, a bit scared... well, possibly very scared... that Tara might start preferring Alessio to her. But that was childish, wasn't it? Love stretched. Tara was perfectly capable of loving them both. And thirteen years had to count for something, hadn't they? Having rammed down her own insecurities, Daisy entered the lounge, determined to be mature and reasonable regardless of how Alessio chose to behave.

She was taken aback to find Tara down on her knees in front of the bookcase, extracting the last of a pile of photo albums, most of which were already stacked suggestively at Alessio's feet. She gave her mother an anxious look. 'You don't mind if Dad borrows these for a while, do you? I said he could.'

Thirteen years of Daisy's life were documented in those albums. Daisy felt that her privacy was being cruelly invaded and had to bite back words of dismayed refusal. Those were Tara's records too. What could be more natural than that her daughter should want to share that pictorial account of her childhood with her father?

'I'll look after them.' Alessio's faint smile was sardonic and Daisy registered the fact that he knew exactly how she felt.

Flushed and uncomfortable, she set a cup of coffee in front of him.

'We can go over them together after I come back from my school trip,' Tara told Alessio earnestly as she scrambled up again. ''Night, Mum...Dad.' She stopped in the doorway, grinned widely at both her parents and slowly shook her head in bemusement. 'It sounds so weird to say that, to have you both here...like a real family.'

Daisy shrank deeper into her armchair as the door closed. Why did Tara have to go out of her way to sound like a deprived child within Alessio's hearing? she thought in distress. A *real* family!

'Family...not a concept you ever knew a great deal about,' Alessio murmured. 'So in one uniquely selfish move you thought nothing of denying her her own family.'

Daisy thought of the family who had made her feel like a tarty little adventuress at her own wedding. Everyone had known she was pregnant. Bianca had made sure of that. And Alessio's mother had cried so much that people could have been forgiven for believing that she was attending her son's funeral. Taking the hint, the guests had stopped mouthing good wishes and had offered sympathy instead.

'It wasn't like that,' she countered.

'You know as well as I do that there would never have been a divorce if my father had known that you were still expecting a child. The subject would not even have been broached.'

Daisy thrust up her chin. 'Do we have to keep harping back to the past?'

Brilliant golden eyes rested on her. 'That past formed the present and will undoubtedly alter the future. Did you really think that I could meet my daughter and then walk away from her again? She's tremendous!' Alessio acknowledged, with a sudden surge of appreciative warmth that sharply disconcerted Daisy. 'Half-child, half-woman, and she slides from one to the other between one sentence and the next.'

Her tense mouth softened. 'Yes,' she conceded.

'She's funny and bright and very open... but do you know what I found hardest to take?' Alessio sprang upright and moved restlessly across the room before swinging fluidly back to her, his strong dark face taut. 'At first, it was like she was getting this one big chance to impress me and she was terrified that she might not make the grade. That's why she's exhausted. She's been living on her nerves all day.'

A lump ballooned in Daisy's throat. She focused studiously on her bare feet.

'I believe that I have set her fears at rest. I told her that I would have been there for her from the very beginning of her life had I been offered that opportunity.'

'I can see how popular I'm going to be,' Daisy muttered helplessly, but he wasn't telling her anything she hadn't expected. She was the fall guy in this newly formed triangle. Nothing would be allowed to come between Alessio and his desire to win his daughter's affection.

No excuses would be made for Daisy. He would emerge from the debris of their broken marriage shining white and squeaky clean. After all, Daisy hadn't given him a chance to be a father.

'On the contrary, you will be very popular, Daisy,' Alessio drawled in honeyed contradiction. 'You are about to play a leading role in fulfilling our daughter's painfully obvious desire for a *real* family.'

Her violet eyes were strained. 'I'm more than willing to meet you halfway for Tara's sake. You can see her whenever you like.'

'I expect much more than that from you.'

Daisy paled at that uncompromising assurance and curled her hands together on her lap. 'I know that you'll probably want to fly her over to Italy to meet the rest—'

'Of the cast of the horror movie you mentioned?'

Daisy reddened fiercely, finding that reference ungenerous when she was bending over backwards to be reasonable. 'You have to make allowances for the fact that I never knew that you would feel like this about Tara—'

'And you have to accept that now I've found her I'm not letting go of her again.'

'I am accepting that.'

'And that either you share on my terms or risk getting left behind,' Alessio extended drily.

Daisy struggled to work out what it was he wanted that she had not already offered. 'What are your terms?'

'Another home, two parents and complete security for my daughter.'

For a moment, Daisy looked back at him blankly. Then her sensitive stomach churned. *Two* parents? He could only be talking about marrying Nina Franklin. She vented a hiss of angry disbelief. 'You're planning to marry Nina and fight me for custody!'

'Give me one good reason why I would try to take an already insecure adolescent girl away from the mother she adores and give her a stepmother she would undoubtedly loathe,' Alessio invited with evident impatience.

'You said that if it took you a lifetime you would punish me!'

'Not at the cost of my daughter's happiness.'

Daisy's brain felt as if it was functioning at half its usual capacity. If Alessio was not talking about marrying Nina... But then he hadn't actually mentioned marriage specifically, had he? He had referred to another home and two parents. So what was he talking about? He simply couldn't be talking about what was currently crossing her mind. *That* would be sheer insanity.

'When did you last have a good night's sleep?' Alessio asked.

'I don't remember.'

'It shows. I feel as though I'm banging my head against a brick wall.

'We were talking about Tara.' Daisy was still shaken and embarrassed by the mad thought that had briefly occurred to her and she reached out for her cup of coffee with what she hoped was an air of cool, detached composure.

'I've already made the decision which will best serve all our needs.' Alessio studied her with brooding eyes, his wide, sensual mouth suddenly setting hard. 'We will get married again.'

As her fingers involuntarily loosened their grip on the cup and hot liquid splashed down her jeans, Daisy vented a startled shriek of pain and sprang up, pressing her palms against her burning thighs. Alessio dealt her a

split-second look of raw incredulity and then strode
forward. Snatching her unceremoniously up into his arms
and tumbling her down on the sofa, he proceeded to
unzip and peel down her jeans at speed.

'What are you doing?' Daisy screeched in horror, en-
deavouring without success to evade his determined
ministrations.

'I heard a scream,' Tara intervened. *'Mum...?'*

'Your mother has scalded herself. Where's the
bathroom?' Alessio countered.

Thirty seconds later, Daisy found herself standing in
the bath with Tara aiming the shower head at her bare
thighs to cool the smarting flesh with cold water. Tears
of mortification had now taken over from momentary
tears of pain. Alessio was rustling, tight-mouthed with
disapproval, through a first-aid box crammed with
cosmetics.

'You're really cool in a crisis,' Tara was saying ap-
preciatively to her father. As she took her attention off
what she was doing, the gushing water angled up to
drench Daisy's T-shirt as well. 'I did a first-aid course
last summer but I wouldn't have remembered what to
do so quickly.'

'I'm all right now,' Daisy murmured in desperation,
cringing with embarrassment.

'You need at least ten minutes of that treatment,'
Alessio overruled.

'At least ten minutes. He's right, Mum,' Tara added,
sounding like a little echo.

'It was a very minor scald. The coffee wasn't that hot.'
Daisy was trying somewhat hopelessly to tug the too
small T-shirt down over a pair of minuscule white pants
which were probably transparent now that they were wet.

'You screamed,' her daughter reminded her. 'You scared me!'

'Don't tell me Daisy hasn't done that to you before. She's accident-prone but wonderfully resilient,' Alessio put in reassuringly. 'She came off my motorbike twice without breaking anything.'

'Mum just hasn't got very good spatial awareness,' Tara told him informatively. 'Aunt Janet thinks it's because she was born weeks before she should have been. That's probably why she's so small and skinny as well. It was a real miracle that she survived. I mean *thirty* years ago a lot of premature babies died! I was only a couple of weeks early. It didn't harm me but Aunt Janet said that Mum's development was definitely affected—'

'I thought you were tired,' Daisy slotted into the flood of chatter, feeling older, smaller, skinnier, clumsier and less adequate than she had in years.

'Yes, you should go back to bed,' Alessio agreed, a slight tremor disturbing his smooth drawl. 'I can handle this.'

Daisy wondered if her legs were turning blue. They were numb. The bathroom was freezing cold too. But it was no use; she couldn't block out that shattering announcement one minute longer. 'We will get married again.' Though every rational thought denied that Alessio could have said that, she knew he had said it. And that unapologetic arrogance was at least familiar. Only the last time Alessio had told her that they were getting married Daisy had had no problem with being told rather than asked...

She had been weak with relief and, indeed, it hadn't been very long before she'd begun feeling incredibly happy that she was going to stay on in Italy as his wife and share as many of his waking and sleeping moments as she could possibly manage. Sadly, her sunny belief that Alessio would soon reach that same blissful state of acceptance hadn't lasted much beyond their wedding night, when she had had the poor taste to joke that she felt like Cinderella.

Alessio had looked at her for the very first time as if he could quite happily have strangled her. His wonderful sense of humour had vanished when he'd put that fatal ring on her finger and it had not reappeared. But had she then sown the first seed of his suspicion that she had been plotting all along to acquire a share of the Leopardi wealth? Daisy reflected that she could truthfully put her hand on her heart and assert that the very last thing that had ever been on her mind when Alessio had been making love to her was money...

Daisy emerged from an undeniably erotic reverie to find her T-shirt being whipped off. She emitted a strangled moan of protest just as her equally sodden bra was tugged down her arms. Alessio wrapped a towel round her bare, pouting breasts, met her outraged eyes and said tautly, 'You're cold and wet. I couldn't undress you in front of Tara. It would have embarrassed her.'

He sank down on the corner of the bath and directed the shower head at her shivering legs, and then his smooth dark head angled down and a lean hand settled on her hip to twist her round. 'Where the hell did you get those bruises?' he demanded thunderously.

'On the stairs at the bank.' Daisy was resigned to humiliation now but striving not to show that it mattered.

'Didn't I tell you to watch out?' Alessio gritted. 'Didn't I warn you?'

'Yes... you're *always* right,' Daisy muttered with a speaking lack of appreciation.

He switched off the water and minutely examined her goose-fleshed thighs for patches of scalded pink. 'Do you feel any heat anywhere?' he finally enquired.

'Are you joking?'

'It could have been a lot worse.' It was quite beyond Alessio to admit that he had overreacted.

He lifted her out of the bath and hunkered lithely down to pat her trembling legs as gently and carefully dry as if she were a baby. Daisy submitted, suddenly so choked up by tears that she was undyingly grateful that it was her skinny thighs that had all his attention. Below the discreet cover of the hip-length towel, her wet pants were tugged smoothly down. She didn't notice, for beneath the overhead light Alessio's black hair had the extraordinary iridescent sheen and lure of pure silk and involuntarily Daisy was entrapped by that compulsive view. She wanted to touch those gleaming strands so badly that her fingers tingled and she had to fold her arms tightly because, for a split second, she really didn't trust herself not to surrender to temptation.

It didn't even occur to her to wonder why Alessio was making her stand on one foot and then the other as the damp scrap of lingerie was deftly wafted away, for Daisy was by then in a hot-cheeked fever of self-loathing. Shame was flaming through her in punitive waves. She despised her physical weakness in Alessio's vicinity. What had been excusable at a sexually naïve and besotted seventeen was in no way allowable in a grown woman of thirty. Raw resentment suddenly filled her to overflowing. She couldn't understand how she could still be so disgustingly susceptible. One attack of Alessio ought to have conferred lifelong immunity.

And how dared he come into her home and upbraid her for *her* failings? He had given up on their relationship first, hadn't he? What possible future could he have envisaged for their marriage when he had already been consoling himself with Sophia? Why hadn't she faced him with that fact? But she knew why, didn't she? She couldn't have mentioned that final betrayal without revealing just how deeply she had been hurt by it. And, thirteen years on, she was too proud to expose herself to that extent.

Secure in the belief that she was ignorant of his extramarital activities, Alessio was aggressively determined to load her down with so much guilt that she wouldn't dare to fight back. And why had she not yet said a word about that insane proposition he had made? Marry Alessio again? Always honest with herself, Daisy could think of several things Alessio might be able to persuade her to do in a weak moment, but a second trip to hell and back was definitely not one of them.

'You should be in bed too,' Alessio said very quietly. 'You're exhausted.'

Banging his head against a brick wall...she reflected furiously. Just how much affronted dignity could one effectively portray standing naked in a towel with intimate items of apparel scattered round one's feet? Particularly one intimate item that she didn't even recall being removed! She could almost feel Alessio consciously tempering his powerful emotions to the constraints of the situation. If she hadn't been hurt, she knew he would have been laughing uproariously at what had happened. Instead he was practising tact. She hated him for that even more.

'Tell me you weren't crazy enough to say that we should get married again,' she begged, hugging the towel round herself as if it were a suit of armour.

'We'll discuss that tomorrow.'

'But there's nothing to discuss,' Daisy returned flatly. 'Don't be silly.'

'There *isn't*!' Stalking out of the bathroom, Daisy returned to the lounge and plonked herself down. Why was she now thinking that for the very first time Alessio had taken off her clothes and failed to make the smallest pass? she asked herself. Was there something wrong with her brain? Was she becoming obsessed with sex? He had been very impersonal about it, too, but teeth-clenchingly considerate. He had averted his attention from her naked body. Why had that only made her squirm more? Why did her ego suddenly feel as if it had been weekending in a concrete mixer?

'Daisy...' Alessio breathed tautly.

Daisy rigorously studied the wall to the left of him, and when he moved into that space found another section of wall. 'If you've got something you feel you *have* to say, say it now and get it over with. I have no intention of making myself available tomorrow.'

'Your towel's slipping...'

Her cheeks burning, Daisy snatched the towel higher over the embarrassingly full thrust of her breasts. She fixed accusing violet eyes on him. 'I want you to know that until this evening I truly believed that there was no sacrifice I would not make for my daughter's benefit. But there is one. I would give her every last drop of blood in my body, but I would throw myself under a bus before I would marry her father again!'

'You haven't even taken time to consider the idea,' Alessio returned very drily.

'Time? You think I need time? Are you out of your mind?' Daisy gasped with unhidden incredulity. 'I couldn't face being married to you again!'

A dark surge of blood had risen over Alessio's savagely high cheekbones. He breathed in deep.

'You always did have the sensitivity of a stone,' Daisy condemned shakily, her temper suddenly engulfed by a violent tide of debilitating memory. Slowly she shook her silver head. 'I would be a very wicked woman to deserve that much misery twice in one lifetime. Most people who sin have to die to go to hell but I got my punishment while I was still breathing.'

'That is not very funny, Daisy.'

'It wasn't meant to be.' Daisy stole a reluctant, fleeting glance at him.

Alessio was broodingly still, eyes of aristocratic ice fixed to her with chilling intensity. The temperature had dropped to freezing point.

'I wasn't trying to be rude. I was just being frank,' she protested, intimidated more than she wanted to admit by the chill in the air but determined that he should realise that he had suggested an act of sheer insanity which it would be a complete waste of time to discuss in any greater depth. 'I suppose you feel that if you're willing to make a huge sacrifice for Tara I should be too... and that most women would take one look at you and your bank balance and flatten you in the rush to the altar... but—'

'Not you,' Alessio slotted in grittily.

'Well, been there, done that... grateful to have got out alive,' Daisy said helplessly.

As the heavy silence stretched unbearably, she suddenly scrambled up again. Walking out fast into the hall, she prayed that he would take the hint and leave without argument. 'The next time you collect Tara, maybe you could just honk the horn... and I'd really appreciate it if you could keep any conversations you feel we must have to the phone—'

'When you bolt from reality, *piccola mia*, you literally streak. And it is done with such a complete lack of shame, it takes my breath away,' Alessio drawled with lethal emphasis.

Her face as hot as hell-fire, Daisy dragged open the front door. 'Goodbye, Alessio.'

CHAPTER FIVE

DAISY slammed the door, shot every bolt home and sagged, until she heard movement in Tara's bedroom. Creeping into her own room, she dropped the towel, grabbed up her nightdress, hauled it over her head and dived at supersonic speed into bed.

The door creaked open. 'Mum...?'

Daisy shut her eyes tight and played dead.

'I won't stay long...' Tara promised, making Daisy feel a total heel. 'I just can't sleep.'

Daisy surrendered. 'So what did you think of...Alessio?'

'He's terrific. We talked about just *everything*!' Tara bounced down on the end of the bed and stuck her feet in below the duvet. 'I even asked him about his girl-friend for you!'

'You did what?' Daisy moaned in horror.

'I knew you were dying to know if it was serious. Relax. We don't need to worry about her. Dad's fin-ished with her.'

'Has he? It's none of my business,' Daisy said, but not quite quickly enough.

'Well, I thought it was very much *our* business,' Tara returned with a meaningful look. 'You should see the way women eye him up when you're out with him...it would frighten the life out of you! He's not going to be alone for long and you haven't got time to play hard to get if you want him back. You need to get in there quick!'

Daisy was aghast. 'Tara—'

'Mum, I *know* you still fancy him like mad! That's why you have that photo of him in your purse and read the *Financial Times* and look tragic when I mention him,' Tara reeled off with overflowing sympathy in her eyes. 'But don't worry—I didn't even drop a *hint* to him! I did ask him what he thought of you, though.'

Daisy rolled over and sank anguished teeth into the pillow.

'Well, I mean, if Dad didn't still fancy you even a bit, I thought *we* should know about it now. Mum, he's still single and he hasn't got anyone either! Don't you think that kind of means he's meant to be ours?' Tara pressed, as if she were talking about a stray dog in need of a loving home.

'No, I don't think that,' Daisy mumbled, but she had a terrifyingly inappropriate urge to giggle.

'Dad *said* you would never have got divorced if he'd known about me. He *said* he really loved you but he wasn't much good at being a husband when he was a teenager. He looked dead guilty too,' Tara revealed with a satisfaction she couldn't hide. 'I think you should have told him about me when I was born. If I'd been you, I wouldn't have let him go! It was his *duty* to be with us and he would have got used to being married eventually.'

That was definitely a self-centred Leopardi talking. Daisy's blood was now running cold in her veins. Tara had already decided that she didn't want Alessio as a part-time father and she was far too possessive to want to share him with any woman other than her mother. 'Very open,' Alessio had said of his daughter. Did that mean he had read Tara like a book? Very probably, Daisy conceded.

Alessio was as sharp as a knife. He was also a Leopardi, born to go from cradle to grave in the belief that he had a hotline to heaven and knew the wisest, smartest move in every situation. Had Tara let Alessio see exactly what she wanted from him? Had Alessio's blood run cold too? Had he then appreciated that Tara could be a real, manipulative handful? Was that why he had said they should remarry? If he was that impressionable, Tara would run rings round him.

Tara got off the bed and sent Daisy a cheeky grin. 'I know you're gasping to hear what he said. Dad thinks you're still gorgeous . . . and I think he'd be doing really well for himself getting a second chance with you—'

'It's not going to happen, Tara,' Daisy said as gently and firmly as she could.

'I don't see why not.' Her daughter looked distinctly smug and gave her mother a warm and approving appraisal. 'Lots of men go for you. Why shouldn't he?'

That revealing and explosive dialogue haunted Daisy throughout the next morning. She couldn't keep her mind on her work and found herself drifting off into thoughts of what life might have been like if she hadn't divorced Alessio. Would he have changed after she had had the baby? Would he have wanted her again then? Would he have dumped Sophia and become a faithful husband? Daisy looked out of the window in cynical search of a flying pig or a blue moon.

'You know, there's something different about you this week,' Barry commented, watching her doodle interlocking triangles on her pad. 'You're much more approachable.'

'Barry—'

'Have dinner with me tonight,' he urged, dropping down athletically into a crouch in front of her swivel chair so that they could meet eye to eye. 'I won't lay a finger on you...I promise!'

'Give over, Barry,' Daisy groaned.

'So I used to show off a little when I first started here but that was *three* years ago,' Barry stressed with a winning smile as he reached for her hands. 'I've grown up since then. I don't boast about my one-night stands any more. I know you're not impressed by how fast I drive my Porsche. I think I could even be faithful for you.'

Daisy studied him and experienced a very, very faint stab of remorse. Deep down inside, she had always known why she had loathed Barry on sight. In build, colouring and brash confidence, he reminded her just a little of Alessio as a teenager. Poor Barry. He had been chasing her for so long that it was a running office joke. 'Sorry—' she began.

'Daisy...'

Releasing her fingers, Barry vaulted upright. Daisy might have got whiplash if Alessio hadn't spun her chair round so fast that she saw whirling lights instead.

'Lunch,' Alessio drawled with definite aggression.

'I'm not hungry,' Daisy muttered out of the corner of her mouth as she turned her chair back to her desk. 'Go away...'

'Mr Leopardi?' Barry cleared his throat after a lengthy pause. 'We spoke on the phone last week—'

'You may inform your superior that Miss Thornton won't be returning to work here,' Alessio interposed, smooth as glass. 'She'll be far too busy roasting in the fires of eternity as my wife.'

'Your...your *wife*?' Barry spluttered incredulously.

Ignoring him, Alessio lifted Daisy's slim handbag from the desk and studied it with scepticism. 'Where's all the rest of the junk?'

'Junk?' Daisy's voice fractured as she rose jerkily upright, unable to believe that he had made such an announcement in front of the entire office.

'Daisy, you couldn't get through one day with a purse this tiny. This is for show. Somewhere else there has to be a holding tank for the hundred and one things you have to keep within reach. *Ah...*' With unhidden satisfaction, Alessio reached below the desk and lifted the large, battered leather holdall he had espied. 'Yours? How often do you feed the purse? Hourly? Half-hourly?'

'I'll be back after lunch, Barry,' Daisy said frigidly, striving to regain control of the situation but quite shattered by the manner in which Alessio was behaving. Barry simply gaped at her.

'You won't be,' Alessio drawled, running at speed through the drawers of her desk, extracting a small teddy bear, a single shoe, three fat romantic novels, two hairbrushes and several packets of tights. He stuffed the lot into the leather holdall. 'Have you a coat? One? Two?'

'I'll see to that.' Joyce giggled into the resounding silence and crossed the room to a cupboard, to emerge with two umbrellas, a coat, a jacket and a pair of red stiletto-heeled ankle-boots which had sent Barry into such paroxysms of lust that Daisy had stopped wearing them out of pity.

'I'll be back,' Daisy said defiantly.

'You're not the Terminator,' Alessio dropped in with gentle satire as he curved a hand round her elbow and marched her out into the fresh air, Joyce following in their wake. 'Didn't the toy boy ever figure out how to derail you? Take you by surprise and you're as helpless as a tortoise turned on its back, *cara*.'

'Was it love at first sight?' Joyce prompted with dreamily intent eyes as she passed Daisy's possessions over to the chauffeur.

'Is that when you feel like you've been run over by a tank?' Alessio enquired with a deeply reflective air. 'That magical but gut-wrenching moment when you realise that nothing is ever going to be the same again? It was more like having a very large rock dropped on me from a height. The earth may have moved but I wasn't fast enough on my feet.'

Daisy studied him in disbelief.

'I suppose men feel they have to fight it,' Joyce sighed philosophically. 'But you didn't fight for long, did you?'

'I don't think you want the answer to that one,' Alessio murmured, pressing Daisy into the limousine and tossing her bag in after her.

'How could you embarrass me like that?' Daisy demanded as the car drew away from the kerb. 'How am I supposed to explain all that nonsense you talked?'

'You won't have to. When I said you weren't setting foot in there again I was not joking. I have already acquired a special licence. We can get married on Saturday morning before Tara goes off on her school trip to France,' Alessio explained with immovable calm.

Her lashes fluttered over incredulous violet eyes. 'A special licence? S-Saturday?' she stammered. 'Are you crazy? We're divorced and staying that way!'

'Are you prepared to lose Tara?' Astute golden eyes rested on her enquiringly.

Daisy stiffened. 'Are you threatening me?'

'It was a warning. I'm telling you what may well happen if we *don't* get married and present a united front,' Alessio pronounced with deflating cool. 'You chose to bring Tara up outside the society in which she belongs and her life is now about to change out of all recognition. She is not in any way prepared for that transformation and my family will try to spoil her as much as they spoiled me.'

Daisy dropped her head in surprise at that admission.

'Everything Tara wants, she will receive. You couldn't possibly compete from a distance, any more than you can continue to deny who she is. She's a Leopardi and one day she will be an extremely wealthy young woman. She will have to make major adjustments.'

'I could help her—'

'How could you help if you weren't there? And how quick would you be to blame me if anything went wrong? Tara will need more backup than I can give her. She will need her mother's full support. When she realises how much she has missed out on, you won't find it easy to stay in control when she's abroad and you're still here in London,' Alessio pointed out drily.

He had spelt out realities about Tara's future that Daisy did not want to hear. Her daughter would indeed find the Leopardi lifestyle shockingly seductive. Her grandparents would undoubtedly greet her with open arms. Tara was, after all, one of *them*. All that money and attention might turn the head of even the most stable adult, so what effect might they have on an impressionable teenager? She remembered the Ferrari, Alessio's eighteenth-birthday present, and her stomach turned over sickly.

'You're talking as if Tara's likely to be spending a lot of time in Italy.'

'You won't have much choice about that, Daisy. My father is moving into semi-retirement. While he will retain a consultative position within the bank, I'm taking over our main office in Rome next month,' Alessio imparted. 'I'll only be back in London on business trips after that—'

'But you were looking for a house *here*,' Daisy said involuntarily, struggling to conceal her growing dismay at what he was telling her.

'I was viewing the house on my parents' behalf, not my own. They're looking for a base in London.'

A base, Daisy reflected dizzily. Only a Leopardi could refer to a house that big and expensive as a base. She surveyed Alessio with dazed eyes. It was a welcome escape from the daunting facts he was hammering her with. He looked gorgeous—undeniably and infuriatingly gorgeous. No sleepless shadows beneath *his* eyes and, remarkably, not even a hint of yesterday's strain. His superbly tailored charcoal-grey suit was a spectacular showcase for his lean, vibrantly male physique, but even so Daisy found that she was experiencing a deep craving to see him in a pair of faded, tight jeans again...

Daisy stopped herself dead, guiltily squashing that train of thought. Why should she get all worked up about the fact that Alessio still attracted her? Wasn't that immature and narrow-minded? It was only her hormones which were at fault—natural female promptings accentuated by silly, sentimental memories. Alessio was incredibly sexy... that was all. Her body was tempted but her intelligence was safely in control.

'So you must see that if I am to establish a relationship of any depth with my daughter she will be travelling to Rome on a very regular basis.'

'Hmmm...' Daisy sighed absently, wondering if he remembered the time she had tried to take his jeans off with her teeth... seriously hoping that he didn't.

'I think that you owe both Tara and me the chance to make something out of this mess.'

Daisy nodded and wished she had sat beside him instead of opposite.

'I also want to give Tara what *she* wants, and I would have to be extraordinarily stupid not to know what she wants after yesterday.'

With enormous effort, Daisy fought to reinstate rational concentration and lifted exasperated eyes to his. 'That's what this is all about, isn't it? You let Tara tie you up in knots, didn't you?'

Disorientatingly, Alessio's gleaming dark gaze flared with spontaneous amusement. 'Not at all. When she asked me very loudly in the middle of a crowded restaurant whether I thought I could still fancy her mum, I took it beautifully.'

The challenging slant of Daisy's chin wavered as she slowly turned a beetroot shade, horror striking into her bones.

'It was only half past twelve but I was already waiting for the question,' Alessio confessed lazily. 'Tara has no subtlety. She can't wait for anything either. She just jumps right in and splashes everyone around her. Thirty-two years' experience of Bianca stood me in good stead.'

Daisy was mortified. 'So you guessed what she was trying to do.'

'She was like a suicide bomber forcing herself out on a diplomatic mission. She told me how she had always thought that you and I had a lot in common with Romeo and Juliet.'

Daisy went from mortification to sheer agony. 'Oh, no—'

'How divorce destroys children's lives: that was phase two. She backed that up with several hair-raising horror stories about schoolfriends. I lunched to the accompaniment of tales about spiteful stepmothers and abusive stepfathers. By the time the dessert cart came my appetite was flagging but Tara was putting away enough fuel to stoke a steam engine,' Alessio recalled wryly. 'I was allowed a break until mid-afternoon before she embarked on the problems suffered by children from broken homes.'

'I'm *really* sorry,' Daisy said feelingly.

'She took me step by painful step through subjects such as low self-esteem and abysmal academic achievement—'

'She's top of her class!' Daisy gasped.

'I suspected that. Nobody that determined to make me feel guilty could possibly be lacking in intelligence. And by the end of my indoctrination session the picture was crystal-clear. Tara worships the ground you walk on. You have also attained martyr status while still alive,' Alessio murmured with sardonic eyes. 'The divorce was fifty per cent my fault and fifty per cent the fault of the in-laws from hell. My evil, scheming parents, who sounded remarkably like a twentieth-century resurrection of the Borgias, may not have succeeded in driving you to suicide but then that is only a tribute to the strength of your character.'

Daisy gulped. 'Teenagers can be very melodramatic.'

'There were moments yesterday when I could have shaken you until your teeth rattled in your head,' Alessio confided. 'But the bottom line is that Tara is consumed by a desire to see us reconciled.'

'It's an understandable dream for her to have,' Daisy conceded grudgingly.

'But I want to give my daughter that dream,' Alessio returned with dangerous softness. The limousine had stopped and the chauffeur walked round the car to open Daisy's door for her. Tight-mouthed, Daisy slid out. 'Where on earth are we going?'

'My apartment.'

Inside the lift, she breathed in deep. 'Alessio... I love Tara very much and I understand that, the way you're feeling right now, you'd try to give her the moon if she asked for it, but I don't want—'

'What you want doesn't come into this.'

Daisy's generous mouth fell wide open.

'Haven't you had everything *your* way for long enough?'

Daisy froze in shock.

'When the going go too rough, you walked out on our marriage without hesitation,' Alessio delivered with aggressive bite. 'I got no choice then and I got even less choice when it came to my rights as a parent. You didn't compromise your wants and wishes until Tara gave you a guilty conscience. If she had had no interest in her absent father, I would probably never have learnt that I had a daughter. *Dio*...I feel I've earned the right to make some demands of my own!'

Daisy was devastated by that condemnation. Clearly, Alessio saw her as an utterly selfish individual who had caused unlimited damage. But she was being unfairly judged by adult standards. In marrying her at nineteen, Alessio had acknowledged that their child's needs should come first. It had been a fine and noble ideal but he had not carried through with the reality that their marriage would have to work to make that possible.

His penthouse apartment was breathtaking. Inquisitively she glanced through open doorways, taking in glimpses of richly polished wooden floors, magnificent rugs and gleaming antiques. In an elegant dining-room, the first course of their meal already awaited them. A silent man-servant pushed her chair in, shook out her linen napkin and poured the wine before leaving them. Daisy emptied her glass fast. Over the rim, she collided with Alessio's broodingly intense dark gaze and the silence pulsed and pounded like the quiet before the storm.

Alessio expelled his breath in an impatient hiss. 'When we met again, I admit that I was very hostile.' His strong jawline squared. 'But that was self-defence. All the memories came back and I only allowed myself to recognise two reactions—lust and anger.'

In the past, Daisy had had a large personal ac-quaintance with both emotions, although, admittedly, Alessio had never before acknowledged the existence of either. She surveyed her empty glass with a sinking heart. She wondered what it would take to satisfy the Leopardi need for blood and retribution. When would Alessio take account of his own sins of omission?

'But there was a lot of pain and bitterness in there too.'

Daisy experienced enough of a surge of interest and surprise to look up and pay closer attention.

Alessio's gaze was screened to a mere glimmer of gold. 'I was amazed that I could still remember those feelings,' he admitted tautly. 'But then my ego was very fragile at the time and you do hold the distinction of being the only woman who ever ditched me for a large injection of cash.'

Daisy's breath caught in her throat as she belatedly recalled that she had not yet explained about that money. 'I—'

Alessio shifted a lean, autocratic hand to silence her. 'But that sordid reality does not release me from what is patently my duty of care and responsibility towards my daughter. Nor do your personal feelings release you from that same obligation.'

Sordid reality? In the midst of reflecting that it might well have done Alessio a great deal of good to believe that he had been ditched in return for a large injection of cash, Daisy was sidetracked by his horrific use of that word 'duty'. Her daughter had used it last night and it had given her mother a distinctly nasty turn. Leopardis were heavily into buzz words of the 'duty' and 'honour' variety. Employing such terms, they braced themselves to do masochistic things and then took revenge by punishing the unfortunate being who had forced them into those sacrifices.

That was the story of their first marriage in a nutshell, Daisy conceded with an involuntary shudder. Alessio had been punishing her for *his* sacrifice. She was not crazy enough to give him a second bite at the same apple. Tara would thank neither one of them for involving her in the misery of an unhappy marriage. If Alessio wanted a sacrifice, he was not going to find one in Daisy. Whatever he might think, Daisy knew she was not good martyr material.

'Daisy...' Alessio breathed in a charged undertone. 'Are you listening to me?'

Like a mouse slowly raising its gaze to risk the hypnotic and deadly enchantment of a snake, Daisy lifted her head. 'Sorry?' she said very tautly.

Anger glittered in his incisive scrutiny. 'No doubt it will surprise you, but I am accustomed to attention when I am speaking.'

Daisy was not at all surprised. Alessio had the most gorgeous dark, seductive drawl. That rich voice sent tiny, delicious quivers down her spine. He also had the most incredibly beautiful eyes and the most fabulous bone structure, she acknowledged, fully concentrating on what really mattered . . . her *own* vulnerability. She could not remarry a man whom she had once loved so much and who had hurt her so terribly. It would be a suicidally stupid act. And she might have a bad habit of learning most of her lessons the hard way but nobody could ever say that she made the same mistake twice!

'But then I am accustomed to dealing with individuals with some *small* measure of concentration,' Alessio added softly.

'This has been a very traumatic week for me,' Daisy muttered evasively.

'Really?' Alessio prompted dangerously, causing her anxious eyes to shoot back to his strong dark face.

'Yes, really.'

'How *could* it have been traumatic?' Alessio thundered in sudden, seething frustration. 'You're on another bloody planet! You might be here in body but you're certainly not here in spirit!'

Daisy reddened with discomfiture. 'I just lost the thread of the conversation for a—'

'What conversation?' Alessio derided. 'You've hardly opened your mouth since we got out of the lift! Barely a word has crossed your lips—'

'I was *listening*,' she protested.

'No, you weren't,' Alessio gritted with a flash of strong white teeth. '*Dio*, how this takes me back! You avoid things that you don't like.'

'I didn't get very far with you, did I?'

Daisy was thinking about the mountain of recriminations that had already come her way. Not a lot to talk about there that she could see. There had been her denial of his parental rights. Fact. Her acceptance of cash in return for him—what other people called a divorce settlement but still fact, since she was technically in possession of that cash. Then there had been the lust and anger bit, followed by the pain and bitterness bit, neither of which had impressed her as being the conversational opener of the year. Alessio took account of only his own feelings and Daisy had not been tempted to reveal what *she* had suffered in the aftermath of their marriage...

Agonies, sheer appalling agonies, she recalled strickenly. She had been like one of those dreadfully clingy vines suddenly torn loose from its only support. Without Alessio, her world had collapsed. Day and night had fused into a progression of endless, miserable hours. If they hadn't kept on remorselessly shovelling food into her in the hospital she wouldn't have survived to tell the tale. But that was not a tale she was about to tell *him*. Wasn't it better that he should believe that she had cheerfully grabbed the money and run? Alessio thought she had departed with a big, brazen, gold-digging bang. Why share the news that she had been one very damp squib?

'Daisy,' Alessio murmured grittily.

But Daisy was still being crushed by the weight of her memories. She had even missed the silences—those volatile, terrifyingly moody silences which had driven her into doormat mode on the least said, soonest mended principle. And yet now she couldn't shut him up, she thought in bewilderment. It was as if he had a mission to talk her to death. Couldn't he understand that she had nothing more to say to him on the subject of remarriage? At least nothing that would not be conducive to further conflict... and Daisy did not like conflict, unless she already had an escape route worked out.

'That's *it*!' Alessio enunciated with grim emphasis.

The Editor's "Thank You" Free Gifts Include:

- ⬤ Four BRAND-NEW romance novels!
- ⬤ A lovely simulated cultured pearl necklace!

YES!

I have placed my Editor's "Thank You" seal in the space provided above. Please send me 4 free books and a lovely simulated pearl necklace. I understand I am under no obligation to purchase any books, as explained on the back and on the opposite page.

106 CIH A7ZL (U-H-P-06/97)

Name _____

Address _____ Apt. _____

City _____

State _____ Zip _____

Thank You!

Harlequin Reader Service® — Here's How It Works:

Accepting free books places you under no obligation to buy anything. You may keep the books and gift and return the shipping statement marked "cancel." If you do not cancel, about a month later we will send you 6 additional novels, and bill you just $2.90 each plus 25¢ delivery per book and applicable sales tax, if any.* That's the complete price, and—compared to cover prices of $3.50 each—quite a bargain! You may cancel at any time, but if you choose to continue, every month we'll send you 6 more books, which you may either purchase at the discount price...or return to us and cancel your subscription.
*Terms and prices subject to change without notice. Sales tax applicable in N.Y.

BUSINESS REPLY MAIL
FIRST-CLASS MAIL   PERMIT NO. 717   BUFFALO, NY

POSTAGE WILL BE PAID BY ADDRESSEE

HARLEQUIN READER SERVICE
3010 WALDEN AVE
PO BOX 1867
BUFFALO NY 14240-9952

NO POSTAGE
NECESSARY
IF MAILED
IN THE
UNITED STATES

Daisy flinched as he thrust back his chair and sprang upright. 'Can I go back to work now?' she asked in a small and not very hopeful voice.

Alessio spread his lean brown hands wide in a frustrated arc. His smouldering golden gaze sizzled across the room and landed on her quailing figure like forked lightning. 'No, you may not go back to work!'

'There's no need to shout—'

'It's shout or strangle you!'

Daisy stood up. 'I was listening.'

'How much did you take in?'

'Were you expecting me to take notes?' Daisy demanded defensively.

In the act of leaving the room, Alessio stopped dead, his broad shoulders rigid. The atmosphere was electric.

'Hang on every word the way I used to?' Daisy continued with unconcealed rancour.

'Even then your mind wandered places I could never follow,' Alessio acknowledged gruffly without turning his head. 'We are very different people.'

For some peculiar reason that reminder distressed her, yet it was an undeniable truth. Alessio was an extrovert, but he didn't show his emotions—not the private ones anyway—and he was always in control. Daisy was an introvert, but love had smashed her barriers and she had poured out on Alessio all the fierce emotion and affection that no one else had ever wanted from her. *She* had been dangerously out of control. Afterwards, she had promised herself that she would never bare herself to another human being like that again. And, with the single exception of her daughter, she had kept that promise.

'Yes...' she acknowledged unevenly, and just in case he might be thinking of that humiliating inequality she

added, 'You're organised and practical and sensible. You
don't lose things or forget things or... or fall over or
off things.' Sucking in a shaky breath, Daisy pinned her
lips shut with an effort, her eyes suddenly smarting with
tears. At seventeen she had been dumb enough to think
that those differences meant that they complemented
each other.

'Exasperatingly efficient but with not much in the way
of imagination?' Alessio queried silkily. 'Possibly I am
about to surprise you.'

'Surprise me?' Daisy questioned.

He swung back another door and stood back for her
to precede him. Her fine brows knit as she walked
through and glanced round a room obviously used as an
office. She cleared her throat uncertainly. 'Why have you
brought me in here?'

His strong dark face hardened. 'I didn't want to have
to do this, Daisy.'

Goose-flesh prickled at the sensitive nape of her neck.
'Do what?'

'It was not my intention to use undue pressure.'

'Undue pressure?' Daisy queried slightly shrilly,
already calculating the distance she was from the door,
her fertile imagination running riot.

'I have employed every means of rational persuasion
within my power.'

'Tara...' Daisy sighed limply.

Alessio lifted a thick document from the desk and held
it out to her.

Daisy tensed even more. 'What's that?'

'A deed of purchase for Elite Estates. I have bought
the agency.'

The taut silence thrummed in her eardrums.

Her brow slowly furrowed. 'That's not possible. Old Mr Dickson would never sell. It was his first business, and he may not take much of a direct interest these days but—'

'The agency is not very profitable given the current state of the property market,' Alessio returned levelly. 'Lewis Dickson couldn't close with my offer fast enough.'

'But what would you want with a London estate company?' Daisy looked at him in perplexity. 'You *couldn't* have bought the agency!' she argued with sudden conviction. 'Giles would have known if there was anything like that in the wind.'

'Carter is only an employee.'

'But he manages Elite Estates—'

'That does not grant him automatic access to his employer's decisions, and discretion was part of the deal.'

Alessio had bought the agency? Daisy studied the document, intricate legal terms blurring beneath her searching gaze until she finally picked out sentences that had a frightening ring of reality. 'I just don't understand why...' she muttered in a daze.

'I *could* make a very tidy profit on the deal. The agency is sitting on a prime site with a great deal of expensive space wasted on that car park. It's ripe for redevelopment.'

'Redevelopment?' Daisy repeated sickly. 'Are you talking about closing the agency down?'

Glittering eyes rested intently on her. 'That's up to you.'

'*Me?*' Daisy gasped. 'What's it got to do with me?'

'The fate of your former colleagues is in your hands,' Alessio delivered softly. 'If you marry me, the agency will continue to do business. If you don't marry me, I will be consoled by a large profit but the agency will cease trading.'

A brittle laugh of disbelief was torn from Daisy. 'You're not serious!'

'Never before has so much ridden on the back of one little deal,' Alessio responded with complete cool.

'But...but *you* wouldn't do that sort of thing...make it personal like that,' Daisy reasoned unsteadily. 'That would be unethical.'

Alessio's eyes met her expectant gaze in a head-on collision. 'Blackmail *is* unethical.'

Daisy tried and failed to swallow at that unashamed acknowledgement. 'You're saying that if I don't marry you you'll put people out of work and it will be my fault. Why... why do you think that will influence me?'

Alessio's gaze wandered over her, taking in her stark white face, the horror in her expressive eyes, and the hold she had on the desk to stay upright. His lush dark lashes lowered and his shapely mouth quirked. 'I know you.'

'You don't know me. If you're the new owner of Elite Estates, it's got nothing to do with me!' Casting aside the document, Daisy turned her back on him, her stomach twisting. She was reeling with shock but struggling desperately hard to hide it.

'Daisy, you couldn't sleep knowing that you were responsible for *one* person losing their job.'

Daisy flinched from that confident assurance, inwardly counting up the ten other people who formed the agency staff. In recent times, many estate agencies had cut back on employees. It would be very difficult, if not impossible for some of her colleagues to find work elsewhere. Four of the men had families to support. One woman was a single parent like herself, another had a husband who had recently lost his own job. The sudden loss of their pay cheques and their security would devastate all their lives.

'Daisy...you feed stray animals. You weep over soppy movies. You worry that plants feel pain,' Alessio enumerated softly. 'That bleeding-heart sensitivity may not have extended to me thirteen years ago but you are definitely not one of the world's most ruthless women.'

'I hate you,' Daisy mumbled strickenly, her slight shoulders rigid with strain.

'You hate spiders...but have you ever stepped on one?'

'Don't be snide.'

'I was being realistic on your behalf.'

'I am a very realistic person but I never, ever thought that you would do anything like this,' Daisy confessed chokily. 'I always thought that aside from all the flaws you couldn't help or were just born with...well, that you did at least *try* to be a basically decent human being...and even if you weren't very good at it at least the trying had to count for something. To find out that you're not even *trying* any more... Well, words just fail me...'

They appeared to fail Alessio as well because the silence stretched and thrummed for enervating and endless seconds. Then a strangled little hiss of air escaped him and all of a sudden he went off into a bout of coughing.

'I hope you choke,' Daisy said thinly while she toyed wildly with the idea of telling Tara about his threat. Her daughter would be appalled. Didn't Alessio appreciate that? If Daisy talked, Tara's trust in her father would be destroyed. But such an act would damage and hurt her daughter most of all, wouldn't it? Tara had so many hopes and expectations already centred on Alessio.

Acknowledging defeat, Daisy sagged like a beaten but bitterly resentful rag doll down into an armchair.

'You've won...'

Alessio swung back to her.

'I'll marry you,' she whispered jerkily. 'But I want you to know that you are making a very big mistake.'

Alessio was very still, not a muscle moving in his darkly handsome face. 'I don't think so.'

'We will be utterly miserable together,' Daisy forecast.

'That's a risk I'm prepared to take.'

'Tara will be miserable too,' Daisy stressed.

'Not if I have anything to do with it.'

'She just won't believe that we're getting married again this fast.'

'No?' Alessio queried silkily. 'I wonder who it was who first filled her head with all that stuff about Romeo and Juliet?'

Daisy flinched and looked hunted.

'Because, oddly enough, she's a very practical girl,' Alessio continued smoothly. 'I wouldn't have said that she had a natural bent for throbbing melodrama. None of my family have. In fact the *only* person I have ever known who could turn a broken cup into a stirring six-act tragedy is—'

'So we're getting married on Saturday, are we?' Daisy broke in feverishly fast.

'But we'll still be lagging a long way behind the example set by Shakespeare's star-crossed lovers.' Alessio contrived to look simultaneously soulful and sardonic. '*They* got hitched within twenty-four hours.'

Two spots of scarlet now burned over Daisy's cheekbones. 'I wouldn't know. I've never read *Romeo and Juliet*,' she said, crossing two sets of fingers the way she always did when she lied.

'I'm reading it line by line. So far, it has been a most enlightening experience.'

Daisy's soft mouth compressed and she tilted her chin. 'This will be a marriage of convenience, right?' she prompted snappishly.

'Mutual convenience,' Alessio agreed silkily. 'What else?'

CHAPTER SIX

JANET and Tara chattered cheerfully the whole way to the register office. It was just as well. Daisy was not in a chatty mood. Her wedding day. Her second wedding day. She tried hard to concentrate on positive thoughts. She was not in love with Alessio, nor did she have any illusions about this marriage. Alessio had made no attempt to pretend that it would be anything more than a convenient arrangement for Tara's benefit.

And Tara was ecstatic, Daisy reminded herself. Indeed her daughter had decided that her father was madly romantic and impetuous and that her mother was one incredibly lucky woman. But then Tara had been so absorbed in the end of the school term, packing for her French trip and contemplating the new life awaiting her in Italy on her return that she was currently suffering from a severe case of over-excitement.

Janet had remarked that Daisy had never been remarkable for her caution in Alessio's radius. As a thought for the day, it had not been inspiring. And when her aunt had had the insensitivity to point out that, after all, she had always had this *thing* about Alessio and that it would be pointless to interfere when the two of them had always acted *crazy* around each other Daisy had almost choked on her sense of injustice.

This time around, she had withstood Alessio with the heroic self-denial of a chocaholic on a strict diet. When he had asked her to marry him again, it had been like a shot of aversion therapy. No blissful dream of drifting down the aisle to the tune of a heavenly chorus had afflicted her. She had felt *ill*, hadn't she? She had not been tempted. But Alessio had employed blackmail. Alessio had defeated her only with cold-blooded threats and intimidation.

And Daisy had been truly shattered by that development. Now she asked herself why. All that inquisitive reading of the financial papers over the years had taught Daisy that Alessio was not a pussy-cat in the business world. Indeed, he was downright ruthless. In the world of international finance, the name of Leopardi was feared as much as it was respected. But the idealistic teenager whom Daisy remembered would never have sunk to using such brutal tactics in a personal relationship.

But then there was no *personal* relationship between them, Daisy acknowledged painfully. Before Alessio had learnt that she had his daughter, he had made it very clear that he wanted nothing more to do with his ex-wife. The sofa encounter had just been the knee-jerk response of an innately sexual predator. It had meant nothing. In fact, Alessio had been eager to believe that she was in his office to scrounge money, because he would have happily *paid* her to go away and lose herself again! So how could she feel anything but bitter and humiliated at the prospect of becoming his wife a second time?

'You're awfully quiet, Mum,' Tara finally observed as Daisy clambered shakily out of the limousine which Alessio had sent to pick the three of them up.

'Wedding-day nerves,' Janet commented lightly.

Tara frowned at her mother. 'I wish you hadn't worn that black suit.'

'It's smart,' Daisy muttered.

'But you look like a pencil going to a funeral.'

A pencil, Daisy reflected wretchedly. She had barely eaten and slept for a week now and it showed. Alessio strolled towards them and her haunted eyes trailed over him in wondering disbelief. He exuded vibrant energy in surplus waves, his eyes diamond-bright, a brilliant smile curving his relaxed mouth. In an exquisitely tailored cream suit that accentuated his golden skin and black hair, he looked as if he had strayed off a Hollywood movie set. Daisy averted her attention again, menaced by the strength and resilience of the enemy.

'As you can see, Mum is just overwhelmed,' Tara burbled. 'It's nerves...not cold feet or anything like that!'

'So you didn't try to make a last-minute break for it through the bathroom window?' Alessio murmured softly to Daisy.

Daisy sidled off one foot onto the other because, oddly enough, there *had* been an insane moment when Tara had been hammering on the door and telling her that the limo had arrived when she had considered using the fire escape. Alessio curved what felt like an imprisoning arm of steel round her slender back. Daisy went rigid. The scent of him so close flared her nostrils. Clean and warm and very male but, worst of all, agonisingly familiar. Her senses remembered him. In a pitch-dark room, she could have picked Alessio out of a hundred men. The knowledge absolutely terrified her.

The marriage ceremony was brief. A tide of sick dizziness ran over her as a slender platinum wedding ring was threaded over her knuckle.

'Signora Leopardi...' Alessio carried her ice-cold fingers smoothly to his lips and kissed them.

The return of that name churned up Daisy's stomach. Tugging free of his light hold, she rubbed her trembling fingers against her skirt. Her wavering smile, kept in valiant place for Tara, died away altogether.

Alessio swept them off to an early lunch at the Ritz. He ate a hearty meal, whereas his bride couldn't manage a single lettuce leaf. He cracked jokes with Janet and teased Tara. No, there was nothing remotely sensitive about Alessio, Daisy reflected. When Alessio triumphed, he was never tempted to a show of mock humility. No, indeed. He radiated glowing satisfaction and that burning, wolfish smile flashed out with unnerving frequency. When a Leopardi was on top, all was bliss in the Leopardi world.

Repelled by that brazen lack of remorse, Daisy escaped to the cloakroom and, finding a comfortable chair, sat there for a while with the attitude of an earthquake victim waiting for the tidal wave that would surely follow. When she finally emerged again, she was startled to find Alessio waiting outside for her.

'I thought you might have done a runner,' he confided with complete calm. 'Lucky for you that you didn't. I would have called the police—'

'The *police*?' Daisy repeated in horror.

'When your sense of tragedy overpowers you, you are very likely to fall under a bus. *Dio*, in the state you're in right now, it would be like letting a rampaging toddler loose in rush-hour traffic!' Alessio said with rueful amusement. 'I have known people who have faced death with greater fortitude than you faced our wedding with today, but it has been a memorable experience for which I thank you from the bottom of my heart. I have been entranced from the minute you tottered into the register office in unrelieved black. Every lachrymose sigh, every sensitive shudder has held me mesmerised.'

Hot pink invading her extreme pallor, Daisy straightened her slight shoulders. 'Excuse me?'

'Oh, don't stop drooping,' Alessio pleaded, studying her with dancing golden eyes. 'It makes me feel so wonderfully medieval and macho.'

'I was not *drooping*!' Daisy bit out in outrage.

'And you look so incredibly feminine and fragile when you do it, I get this really erotic buzz,' Alessio drawled with thickened emphasis, his golden eyes flashing over her with a sudden, startling smoulder of raw sexual appreciation.

Shocked to the core by the unexpectedness of that assertion, Daisy connected with that explicit look and jerked as if she had been struck by lightning. Instantaneous heat surged up inside her, making her slender thighs clench. Suddenly it was alarmingly difficult to breathe and her heart was pounding insanely fast. Horrified, she dropped her head, breaking that dangerous visual contact while she struggled to still her racing pulses and conceal the response he had so effortlessly evoked.

'That remark was inappropriate,' Daisy managed to say in what she hoped was a lofty tone of disapproval. 'This is a marriage of convenience.'

'Convenience.' The repetition deep and audibly appreciative, Alessio caught her hand smoothly in his to lead her in the direction of Tara and Janet, who stood across the foyer. 'How do you define convenience, or haven't you got around to that yet?'

'Separate bedrooms,' Daisy said in breathless clarification. 'I should think that was obvious.'

'Barry was *so* sweet last night,' Tara was proclaiming loudly as they drew level. 'I felt really sorry for him. He even brought Mum flowers.'

Alessio stilled. 'Barry?'

Spinning around, Tara flushed and threw her father a startled look.

Daisy stiffened. 'He called in to see me... and wish me well.'

Out of her daughter's hearing, Barry had congratulated Daisy on being such a fast mover and had then implied that she owed him a favour for her good fortune as Alessio had, after all, been his client. 'Maybe you would like to marry him instead,' Daisy had said. Barry had roared with laughter and soon revealed the true motivation behind his visit. That very morning, Giles had told Barry that Alessio now owned Elite Estates. Barry, very much in barracuda guise, had called round to remind Daisy that she had always thought Giles Carter was a sexist pig. He had gone on to suggest that young, aggressive blood in management would bear much more profitable fruit.

They dropped Tara off with her luggage at the school. She hurtled onto the waiting coach to join her friends and waved frantically through the back window.

'She's scared that one kid on that coach will fail to see the limousine,' Daisy groaned in embarrassment.

'She's happy,' Alessio countered. 'That's all that matters.'

A few minutes later, the limo drew up outside Janet's house. Her aunt smiled widely at them both, her eyes brimming with wry amusement, her indifference to the tense atmosphere profound. 'Have a wonderful honeymoon!' she urged with immovable good cheer.

'What honeymoon?' Daisy bleated as the door thudded shut.

'We're flying straight to Italy,' Alessio informed her. 'Janet packed a few things for you.'

'What do *we* need with a honeymoon?'

'I think we need one very, very badly.'

'I thought I would be moving into your apartment until Tara got back—'

'But you hadn't packed for that eventuality either, had you?' Alessio murmured drily.

The uncomfortable silence lasted all the way to the airport and onto the Leopardi private jet. After take-off, the steward served them with champagne and offered them the flight crew's best wishes.

'Have you told your family about this yet?' Daisy asked Alessio abruptly.

'Of course.'

'I suppose it hit them harder than a crisis on Wall Street.'

'They would have liked to have attended the wedding.'

Daisy turned as pale as death and helped herself to some more champagne with an unsteady hand. 'And I thought the day couldn't have got any worse...'

'There would have been no recriminations,' Alessio asserted.

Daisy sat forward, dragged from her lethargy by a horrible thought. 'We're not going back to live with them, are we?'

Alessio expelled his breath in a hiss. 'Of course not!'

Daisy sank back, weak with relief.

'But they were extremely shocked to learn that I am the father of a teenage daughter,' Alessio admitted tautly. 'They feel very guilty.'

Daisy wasn't listening. She had already switched off. One Leopardi at a time was enough for her to deal with. 'This has been the very worst week of my life,' she complained, looking back on a mindless blur of sleepless nights, abandoned meals and thumping tension headaches.

'Last Saturday, I met you again. It destroyed my weekend,' Alessio volunteered with velvet-smooth emphasis. 'On Monday, you told me I was a father. I spent the night walking the floor. Tuesday was dominated by an almost overwhelming desire to seek you out and strangle you. I consoled myself by buying the estate agency. Wednesday, I met my daughter. I cooled down and started to laugh again. Thursday, I had to play games of entrapment. Friday, I prayed that Tara would prevent you from buying a one-way ticket to somewhere like the Bermuda Triangle. But today we got married and the games are over. I can now finally relax.'

Outraged by that assessment, Daisy studied his darkly handsome face and long, lithe, undeniably indolent sprawl. 'How can you call what you did to me a game? You *blackmailed* me!'

Alessio surveyed her, his bright gaze a sliver of gleaming gold below luxuriant ebony lashes. 'Stress is not for you, *piccola mia*. I thrive on it. You don't. If I hadn't gone for the special licence and the blackmail you might well have starved yourself into a lasting decline before I got you to the altar. You've already lost a lot of weight.' His lean features were surprisingly taut.

The complete exhaustion which Daisy had been fighting off all week was relentlessly gaining on her. It was becoming an effort to think straight. An enormous yawn crept up on her while she wondered why he was going on about her weight.

'And let me assure you that you will not be staging a continuing decline under any roof of mine. The next meal that is put in front of you you will eat,' Alessio spelt out as he sprang lithely upright. 'Now I think you should get some rest.'

Daisy regarded the ring on her finger with a heart that sank, and then looked up. 'You're trying to manage me. I don't like being managed. I don't like being married either,' she added helplessly.

'We have only been married for five hours.' A slow, teasing smile curved Alessio's sensual mouth as he gazed down at her.

It was the most genuine smile that Alessio had given her over the past week but Daisy was even more chilled by the charismatic approach. Tara smiled just the same way when she was after something—usually something that cost two arms and a leg. 'Five hours feels like long enough.'

'When a challenge comes knocking on the front door, you're already halfway out the back, aren't you? You're faster on your feet than a greyhound!' Alessio censured her grimly as he bent down and without the smallest warning scooped her bodily out of her seat. 'You've done that from the first night we met, right through our marriage and out of it again, and you were still doing it this week when you bolted from the bank. But there'll be no escape *this* time, I assure you.'

'What do you think you're doing?' she gasped, unnerved by his behaviour.

'What I should have done an hour ago. You're suffering from sleep deprivation.' Alessio laid her down on the bed in the cabin. 'Trying to talk to you now is like trying to talk to a drunk. I am getting nowhere fast. And it's all my own fault. *Mea culpa.* I employed every device

I could to nail you. I leant on your conscience. I crowded you. Your weaknesses were my strengths. I admit it. Does that make you feel better?'

Dumbstruck, Daisy stared up at him.

Alessio sank down on the edge of the mattress and calmly took off her shoes. 'One bad week and we're married. What's one bad week?'

'It was fourteen the last time . . . hell on earth—'

'It was not hell on earth. *Dio*, give me strength!' Alessio growled, searing her with exasperated eyes. 'So we had a few problems . . . OK? But it wasn't all my fault. You changed. All of a sudden you were creeping about like Little Orphan Annie, looking all wounded and pathetic.'

'You stopped talking to me.'

'I wasn't talking to anyone.

'You could have talked to me.'

'You couldn't have handled it. You were blissfully oblivious to the fact that life as I knew it had gone down the tubes.' A wry smile twisted his well-shaped mouth and then faded again. 'Superficial things that shouldn't have mattered to me *did* matter then. My friends thought it was hilarious when you ended up pregnant. In fact, they thought it was the funniest thing they had ever heard. Alessio had finally got caught.'

Daisy winced and paled. 'I didn't know that.'

'And anything *but* marriage would have been cool in my circle. I wasn't very good at laughing at myself at nineteen. One day I was a social lion, the next a hermit . . . and then on top of that I had Vittorio trying to act the heavy father for the first time at the wrong time . . . you weeping over me, my mother weeping over me, Bianca weeping over me. You're right,' Alessio suddenly breathed, with the faintly dazed air of one making a long-unacknowledged admission. 'It *was* sheer bloody hell.'

Daisy flipped over and looked at the wall. Her eyes stung, her mouth quivered. He was finally agreeing that their first marriage had been a nightmare. She felt astonishingly ungrateful for that agreement. Why was it that she should now recall odd little moments when the sheer hell seemed worth it? She was being very perverse. And at seventeen she must have been appallingly self-centred not to appreciate that Alessio might be suffering just as much as she was, if not more...

As she lay there, Daisy saw the past slowly rearrange itself along less familiar but perhaps more realistic lines, and it was not a pleasant experience. Alessio might have changed towards her but hadn't she also changed towards him? The sunny romantic he had shared that summer with had turned into a weepy wet blanket. She *had* been a complete pain. Wasn't it time she admitted that? Out of her own emotional depth and feeling painfully insecure, she had needed the kind of constant reassurance that no teenage boy would have been capable of giving her.

Alessio had not been deliberately punishing her. He had been getting by the only way he could. He had even tried to protect her by keeping quiet about his own problems. His friends laughing at him... Daisy shrank from that image, remembering with aching clarity just how proud Alessio had been then. It must have taken real guts to marry her in the face of that cruel adolescent mockery. His friends would have been far more impressed if he had given her the money for a termination and put her on the next flight back to London. She swallowed back the thickness ballooning in her throat.

And if Alessio had blamed *her* for just about everything that had gone wrong between them, hadn't she been guilty of doing the exact same thing to him? When had she ever looked back and acknowledged that she had made mistakes too? She had dug her head into the sand and hoped and prayed that their problems would magically melt away. Paralysed by the fear that she was losing him, she had done nothing constructive either, she reflected with growing discomfiture.

'Alessio...?' Daisy whispered thickly, and then, frowning, she turned her head.

But Alessio had already gone, leaving her alone. Just as quickly the past lost the power to hold her. It was the present which was tearing her apart. Alessio could freely admit to having forced her back into marriage and yet his conscience remained clear. In his view, she had committed a far greater sin in denying him all knowledge of his child. And as Tara's mother she was merely a useful adjunct to Alessio's desire to have full custody of his daughter. As a woman, as a wife, she didn't count.

With that depressing thought, Daisy fell asleep.

A hand on her shoulder shook her half-awake. Daisy focused blearily on the photo album lodged mere inches in front of her face.

'Who is that?' Alessio enquired, a lean finger indicating the male standing beside her and a three-year-old Tara in one of the photos.

Daisy made an effort to concentrate. 'That was George—'

'And this character?' Alessio flipped over a page.

Daisy focused uncertainly on another male face. 'Daniel...I think.'

Another page turned. A giant yawn crept up on her as she peered at the handsome blond man whom Alessio was now indicating. She looked blank. 'I don't remember him—'

'You don't remember him? I'm not surprised!' Alessio blistered down at her, making her jump in shock. 'Tara gave me six albums. Every one of them is full of strange men! You could run an international dating agency out of the male contingent in your photographs!'

Daisy gazed up at him with wide, drowsy eyes filled with incomprehension.

'Tara told me that you didn't date, that you hardly ever went out...'

Daisy's sleepy eyes opened even wider. She was shocked that her daughter could have told such a whopper. She had always enjoyed a reasonably healthy social life.

With a not quite steady hand, Alessio snapped the offending album shut. 'I suspected a certain amount of exaggeration on that point.' Scorching golden eyes raked her small, sleep-flushed face accusingly. 'But I had *no idea* what she was covering up! What about the toy boy?'

'Toy boy?' Daisy repeated dazedly, hanging on every explosive word that emerged from between his bloodless, compressed lips.

'He was the latest, wasn't he?' Alessio surveyed her with sudden, icy derision, anger reined in as his expressive mouth clenched as hard as a vice. '*Dio*...you've been sleeping around ever since you divorced me!'

As the door slammed on his exit, Daisy's jaw dropped. Sleeping around? Was he crazy? Sex had just about wrecked her life at seventeen and she had learnt that lesson well. Casual intimacy was not for her. She might have had no shortage of male company over the years

but she had never fallen in love again—hadn't wanted
to either, she acknowledged honestly—and it had always
seemed easier to end relationships when they'd demanded more than she'd been prepared to give.

Janet, she reflected drowsily, might say that she had
a fear of commitment that amounted to paranoia, but
she herself thought that she had been very sensible. No
man had caused her grief in thirteen years. She was proud
of that record and not at all proud of the fact that she
had been a mass of painful and grieving nerve-endings
from the instant that Alessio had come back into her
life.

Daisy shifted in voluptuous relaxation. The bed was very
comfortable. Memory slowly stirred. A slight frown-line
divided her brows. She had the oddest recollection of a
meal being thrust under her nose when being forced to
stay awake had felt like the cruellest torture. She had
pleaded for the mercy of a bed.

And had Alessio really said, 'If you don't eat, you
don't sleep,' and cut up a steak into tiny, bite-sized pieces
while her head had sunk back down on the supporting
heel of her hand and her eyelids had kept on closing no
matter how hard she tried to keep them open? He had
been so damnably domineering, but the chocolate gateau
which had come next had melted in her mouth and for
the first time in a week her stomach had felt settled instead of queasily empty.

They were in Italy... and Alessio was smouldering
again but, unhappily, *not* in silence, she thought as she
recalled that scene with the photo album. At nineteen,
Alessio had told her that a boy who slept around was
only gaining necessary masculine experience but that a
girl who slept around was a tart. That might not be fair

but that was life, he had informed her cheerfully. But Alessio could not find it within himself to be quite so cheerful now about the idea that he might have *married* a tart.

Daisy might have told the reassuring truth had she been asked, but she hadn't been asked. Alessio was not prone to demanding direct answers on sensitive subjects. He was naturally devious. Being sneaky had put him into the hands of his equally sneaky daughter. Tara, bless her scheming and shrewd little Leopardi brain, had worked out exactly what her father wanted to hear and had given it to him in spades. Daisy felt no pity for Alessio. Her sex life...or indeed her lack of a sex life...was none of his business.

But, for her daughter's sake, she had to make the best of this crazy marriage, she told herself staunchly. Thankfully, she was *not* the sort of female who made a six-act tragedy out of a broken cup, contrary to Alessio's opinion. She lifted her feathery lashes and then froze. A stricken gasp was torn from her. All languor banished, Daisy jackknifed upright, her horrified gaze flying round the eerily familiar contours of the spacious room.

Vacating the bed in a flying leap, she wrenched back the curtains with impatient hands and looked out in disbelief at the formal gardens spread out below. Box-shaped parterres adorned with statures and fountains and huge planted stone urns ran up to the edges of a magnificent oak wood. Beyond the trees stretched the rolling verdure of the Tuscan hills.

The very first time Daisy had seen that magnificent view, she had been under the naïve impression that she was having a guided tour of the palatial Leopardi summer home. Alessio's parents had generally been in residence only at weekends. Daisy had been hugely intimidated by her luxurious surroundings. Having got her off balance, Alessio had easily overcome her shy, uncertain protests by smoothly locking his mouth to hers in heated persuasion and sweeping her off to bed to deprive her of her virginity...

But not before assiduously assuring her that he would not go one step further than she wanted him to, that she had only to say no and he would immediately stop. Daisy hadn't been capable of vocalising a single word in the flood of passion which had followed. Alessio would naturally have worked that fact out beforehand. Even as a teenager, he had been ruthlessly well acquainted with her every weakness.

Daisy finally spun from the window and back into the present, trembling with outrage and discomfiture. How dared Alessio bring her back to the family villa in Tuscany? How could any man be so insensitive that he didn't appreciate that this was the very last place she would want to revisit? This was where they had fallen in love, where they had played adult games of passion, blithely risking consequences that neither of them had been equipped to deal with.

She was standing beneath the shower in the adjoining bathroom before it occurred to her that thirteen years ago that bedroom had been *his* bedroom. Of course it wouldn't still be his, she thought, scolding herself furiously for the fact that her impressionable heart had just skipped an entire beat. Instead of being clenched by horror, she had been clenched by excitement, she conceded with deep chagrin. But she would never allow herself to succumb to the potent lure of Alessio's all-pervasive sexuality again. A healthy distance and detachment would provide the only safe and sensible foundation for a marriage of convenience.

Daisy turned off the shower and towelled herself dry. Then, throwing the towel aside, she padded back into the bedroom. She was heading for the dressing room, where she hoped to find some clothing, when a light knock on the door momentarily froze her to the spot. She wasn't wearing a stitch! As the doorhandle began turning, she gave a frantic, unavailing pull at the securely lodged sheet on the bed and then dived with a strangled groan under the massive bed to conceal herself. The rattle of china broke the silence. Daisy waited to see a pair of maid's feet approaching but instead she saw male feet...unmistakably Alessio's feet—bare, brown, beautifully shaped.

'Daisy...?' he called.

She held her breath and turned puce with mortification. Things like this did not happen to other people; why did they continually happen to her? Especially around Alessio, who would greet a hurricane in the middle of the night with a stopwatch. He checked the bathroom, the dressing room, muttered something in Italian.

Daisy couldn't stand the suspense any longer. She cleared her throat. 'I'm under the bed. For heaven's sake, go away!' she hissed in furious conclusion.

'So... you are hiding under the bed,' Alessio drawled after a lengthy pause, a slight tremor disturbing his diction.

'I thought you were the maid.'

'I know you used to feel a little self-conscious around the staff, *piccola mia*...but don't you think this is rather excessive?'

'If you must know, I haven't got any clothes on!' Daisy blitzed back.

'Oh, I'm well aware of that,' Alessio assured her huskily. 'I was standing below the trees earlier when you hauled open the curtains and stood there in all your un-clothed glory for an entire ten minutes.'

'You *timed* me?' Daisy could barely frame the scan-dalised demand.

'I may not wax lyrical about sunrises or spout ro-mantic speeches under balconies but I was deeply ap-preciative of that particular view. I also congratulated myself on my foresight that the domestic staff come in at only discreet hours of the day. We are presently the only people in the house—and isn't it fortunate that I included the gardeners in that embargo? I don't think I'm narrow-minded but I'm remarkably selfish. If you had even unwittingly flashed your attractions for anyone else, I would have wrung your neck!'

'Get out of here, Alessio!' Daisy exploded, fit to be tied.

'But I haven't enjoyed myself this much in years,' Alessio said with intense appreciation. 'Why? I have learnt to cherish and value eccentricity and I am re-joicing in the sure knowledge that my wife is unique. I am certain that I am the only man in Italy who had to force-feed his bride on their wedding night, put her to bed alone and then hold a conversation with her while she hid naked under the bed the next day.'

'*Push off!*' Daisy screeched, unimpressed. 'I'm not coming out until you go away!'

Alessio set down a tray on the carpet. 'Look,' he in-vited in a lazily seductive undertone. 'Your favourite hot chocolate topped with whipped cream. Disgustingly rich and sweet. Every undiscriminating taste bud you possess has to be watering...'

'I don't want it!' Daisy hauled wildly at the sheet hanging over the bed. It still wouldn't budge. Her teeth ground together. Then she espied something cotton lying in a heap on the floor on the other side of the bed and rolled over to stretch out her hand and retrieve it.

'Even when you are concentrating sufficiently to know what's happening around you...which admittedly isn't all that often...you still fascinate me,' Alessio mused reflectively, stretching out long, denim-clad legs as he sank down in an armchair. 'Any other woman would have got *into* the bed to conceal herself but you crawled under it.'

Feverishly engaged in trying to button the shirt, Daisy's fingers slowed to a clumsy fumble as she focused on those legs. She emerged from below the bed, silver hair wildly mussed, her violet eyes as bright as jewels in her triangular face. Treating her to a shimmering smile of blinding brilliance, Alessio sprang fluidly upright, a disturbing distraction in faded tight jeans and a white polo shirt.

Transfixed by that heart-stopping smile, her mind a dizzy blank, Daisy was now wholly absorbed by the jeans. Her mouth ran dry. She moistened her lips, her breath catching in her throat. Denim faithfully followed every superbly virile line of his lean hips and long, powerful thighs. Her magnetised attention strayed to the distinctively masculine bulge at his crotch and something almost painful twisted low in her stomach, colour slowly creeping up her slender throat in a burning wave.

'Do the jeans still make your socks sizzle even when you're not wearing any?' Alessio enquired with purring emphasis as he reached down a strong hand and tugged her upright. '*Dio*, I should have ransacked my wardrobe in London. To hell with sartorial elegance! Clearly I missed out on a critical coup.'

'Rubbish!' But Daisy was convinced that even her toes were turning shocking pink and could not credit that she had gawped at him like that. How could she have? How *could* she have? Her face burned hotter than ever.

'And you are walking a tightrope in that shirt. Tara is not in a bedroom next door. You have no safety net. When you fall... I'll catch you.'

His narrowed gaze was a hot sliver of stark gold, semi-concealed by the lush crescent of his lashes. In the humming stillness, her fingers flew up to the pulse flickering madly at the base of her throat and pressed against it; she frowned as she tore her gaze free and finally registered that she was wearing one of *his* shirts.

'Where did you sleep last night?' Daisy demanded starkly.

'In the dressing room... like a gentleman.'

Her brows knit as she pondered that admission. 'Was there only one bedroom prepared for us?'

'You haven't buttoned my shirt up properly,' Alessio murmured as if she hadn't spoken, and that deep, low-pitched observation made her knees wobble. 'Don't worry about it. I have every intention of taking it off again.'

Her startled eyes whipped back up to his. 'But we're not going to *do* things like that!' Daisy gasped.

'You do have some very peculiar ideas about marriage, *piccola mia*.'

'You only married me to get custody of Tara... it's nothing more than a convenient arrangement!'

'Convenient—available, ready-made, handy,' Alessio defined softly, savouring the words, his brilliant golden eyes smouldering over her with unconcealed anticipation.

'Forget it!' Daisy said furiously, drawing herself up to her full five feet. 'I am not a fast-food outlet...'

Alessio flashed her a megawatt smile of wolfish challenge. 'And I am no celibate. I'm an unreconstructed, very old-fashioned guy. My wife shares my bed. That is not an issue up for negotiation today, tomorrow or any other day. You will not qualify for a separate bedroom should there be fifty guest rooms under the marital roof!'

CHAPTER SEVEN

DAISY was stunned by the sheer challenging cool of that brazen assurance. 'You know that I won't agree to that,' she stated tightly.

Alessio elevated a winged ebony brow. 'No?'

'No. Sharing a bedroom or a bed is out of the question. And I'd like you to leave so that I can get dressed,' Daisy informed him in speedy conclusion.

'Daisy—'

'There's the door. Use it,' Daisy advised, tilting her chin. 'This is not the average marriage. I was forced into it against my better judgement.'

'But whichever way you look at it we're *still* married. And without the passion this marriage hasn't got a hope in hell. In fact right now it's the only damned thing we've got going for us,' Alessio returned very drily. 'So why would you try to deny us that one positive element?'

Unprepared for that raw candour, Daisy lost every scrap of her animation and colour. In demanding a room of her own, she had only been trying to protect herself. She was terrified of putting herself in a position where Alessio could hurt her again. And she could not imagine making love with Alessio without an awful lot of vulnerable feelings becoming involved and putting her at risk.

'I will not allow you to sabotage this marriage before it even gets a fighting chance,' Alessio asserted with stark impatience. 'Just for once in your life you are going to stand your ground and make a real effort.'

125

Daisy snatched in a shaky breath. 'You have no right to speak to me like that.'

His starkly handsome features were set concrete-hard. Icy eyes held hers with an innate force of will. 'It was a warning. No matter how bad things get, you are staying this time. We have Tara to think about now—'

'Yes ... but—'

'And it was a miracle that I didn't drop dead with shock when *you* attacked *me* last week!' Alessio continued with raw emphasis, his lip curling at the memory. 'It took you thirteen years to work up the courage to tell me why you walked out and you slung it all at me as if you were telling me things I already knew!'

Daisy stiffened. 'I—'

'But not one word did you say to me at the time!' Blazing golden eyes raked over her small, still figure. His wide mouth clenched hard, fierce tension splintering from every taut angle of his lean, poised length.

'So, believe it or not, the divorce hit *me* very hard! *I wasn't prepared for it* and *I certainly didn't see it coming*. I loved you and I genuinely believed that you loved me ... and then I found out different, didn't I, Daisy?'

That devastatingly candid admission hung there, quivering in the rushing silence.

Daisy was frozen to the spot, plunged at shattering speed into emotional turmoil. Even that day at the bank, she had not considered the staggering idea that Alessio might *not* have wanted the divorce. 'You're just saying that now to make me feel bad,' she censured him in a faltering undertone. 'You're lying.'

Alessio strode forward. '*Dio*, I—'

Pale and taut, Daisy whirled away from him. 'You're trying to twist everything and act as if I left for no good reason when you know very well that there was nothing left to stay for! You had already moved out of our bedroom!'

Alessio tugged her back to him, his strong hands closing round her slim forearms to imprison her. His dark features were rigid and his eyes held something that looked remarkably like bewilderment. His long fingers tightened on her slender arms and then loosened before slowly dropping from her. His ebony brows drew together, black lashes lowering as he frowned down at her. 'Only because I couldn't sleep in the same bed and hope to keep my hands off you.'

'That doesn't make sense—'

'Doesn't it? The most embarrassing time of my life,' Alessio confided with a rueful twist of his eloquent mouth, 'has to be the day my father cornered me to say that he sincerely hoped that I wasn't still making sexual demands on my wife because pregnant women didn't find lovemaking comfortable after the first couple of months.'

Daisy's jaw dropped.

'I was *seriously* embarrassed,' Alessio admitted with a grim half-smile of remembrance. 'And I wanted to ask you whether I had been hurting you but I couldn't quite work up the courage. My demands in that department had, after all, been pretty voracious—'

'I thought you didn't want me any more,' Daisy interrupted, in a complete daze. 'You never hurt me.'

'Didn't I?'

She shook her head in an urgent negative, her shining silver-blonde hair flying round her flushed cheekbones, her violet eyes welded to his.

'That was why I felt so guilty when you lost the baby,' Alessio confessed harshly. 'I thought that all those passionate encounters might have contributed to that—'

'No!' Daisy protested in a pained whisper, her gaze soft with distress as she drew instinctively closer to him and smoothed her fingers down his arm in a comforting motion. 'That was just something that happened. The doctor had assured me that there was no reason why we shouldn't be making love—'

'How the hell could you have believed that I didn't want you any more?' Alessio broke in with a blatant lack of understanding.

'That's how it seemed. You never touched me again,' she muttered uncomfortably.

'Daisy, I couldn't *trust* myself to touch you! I didn't have any self-control around you and I was very frustrated,' he breathed feelingly. 'Celibacy felt like another punishment. I was a selfish little jerk.'

'No, you weren't,' Daisy said shakily, devastated by what he had told her but undeniably touched too. Her heart skipped a beat as her eyes connected with his vibrant golden gaze. A tiny muscle somewhere deep down inside her pulled tight and her lower limbs turned weak as insidious heat curled in the pit of her stomach. 'But you didn't have to be so extreme...' She swallowed and the tip of her tongue stole out to moisten her full lower lip. 'We could have done—'

'Other things to ease my raging libido?' Alessio slotted in huskily as he reached out and folded both arms round her to ease her up against him, his burnished gaze nailed with magnetic attention to the voluptuous curve of her pink mouth. 'Having made my magnificent gesture of self-sacrifice, I was in full martyr mode, and I was far too proud to come back and ask for favours.'

'It...it wouldn't have been a favour...'

'No?' Alessio prompted thickly.

'I always liked making you lose control…it was almost as exciting as losing it myself,' Daisy confided abstractedly, in severe shock and unable as yet to emerge from it. In one bitter bout of confidence, Alessio had yanked the ground from beneath her feet. All those years ago, he had not turned away from her in deliberate rejection. No, indeed. Incredible as it seemed to her, Alessio had still been seething with unabated lust for her dumpy little barrel of a body, and that thought knocked Daisy sideways and over.

'*Please*…don't say things like that,' Alessio groaned, and with lean, strong hands he gradually drew her up the poised length of his taut, muscular body, letting her find out for herself why he was trembling as she came into head-spinning contact with the bold, hard jut of his aroused masculinity.

Held level with the scorching blaze of his eyes, Daisy hadn't a single thought in her entire head. Every wanton skin cell in her body was busy limbering up at the starting line and Alessio did not disappoint her. He took her mouth with a wild, hot hunger. Excitement hit her in a violent shock wave of response. In an instant, she closed her arms round him, sent her fingers delving blissfully into his luxuriant hair and only uttered an encouraging moan when he sent his hands travelling down over her hips and clamped them to her slim thighs to hold her in place.

That single kiss blazed into fiery heat. Her head spun. Her heart raced. The passion she had damped down and suppressed for too long exploded in a shower of multicoloured fireworks and blew her away. With a muffled growl of raw satisfaction, Alessio hungrily probed her mouth with a wickedly erotic precision that imitated a far more primal possession.

He set her down and flipped her round, his seeking mouth delving in marauding exploration of the soft, sensitive skin between her neck and her shoulder, discovering pulse points she had forgotten existed. Daisy extended her throat in an ecstasy of shivering pleasure and automatically snaked her hips back into the hard, thrusting heat of him, feeling him shudder in urgent sexual response to that helpless provocation.

He brought his hands slowly, caressingly up over the straining thrust of her breasts, their swollen fullness pushing against the smooth cotton of the shirt. As his thumbs brushed and circled over the aching prominence of her nipples, all Daisy's breath escaped at once. Damp heat surged between her trembling thighs and her legs buckled. Twisting her round, Alessio lifted her against him to bring her down on the bed, locking her mouth urgently beneath his again.

'You said I was incredible in bed,' Alessio breathed raggedly, blazing golden eyes holding her entrapped as he sat up and peeled off his shirt. 'It wasn't true. We were incredible *together...*'

As a muscular golden brown expanse of chest highlighted by a triangle of curling black hair filled her vision, Daisy started melting from outside in, languorous weakness enclosing every limb. Alessio leant over her, releasing the buttons on the shirt then spreading the edges apart with deft fingers, to gaze down at the pouting swell of her pale breasts with explicit appreciation.

As their eyes collided again and meshed, Daisy quivered in sensual shock. He lowered his dark head and his mouth engulfed an achingly tender pink nipple, making her jerk and moan in unconscious supplication as her fingers tangled with his hair and then clutched blindly at his shoulders. The sensuous glide of his teeth was followed by the soothing sweep of his tongue. Her breath escaped in torturous bursts, her whole body burning up.

Somewhere irritatingly close a telephone shrilled and she frowned. Alessio cursed with what breath remained to him. Two more rings and a vicious burst of Italian was dragged from him. With the abruptness of violent frustration, he lifted himself away from her and lunged a seeking hand down to retrieve a mobile phone.

Then, unexpectedly, Alessio froze, dark blood highlighting the hard slant of his cheekbones while Daisy watched him in growing fascination.

'Hi,' he murmured with surprising warmth. '*Sì... Sì*... wonderful... terrific... great... Would you like to speak to your mother?'

'Tara?' Daisy mouthed, her embarrassment as instinctive as it would have been had their daughter walked in and surprised them in bed together.

Alessio extended the phone without a word.

'How are you guys getting on?' Tara chattered. 'I knew you'd be worried sick about me because this is the first time I've been away.'

'Yes—'

'Isn't Dad romantic taking you back to where you first met?' Tara gushed. 'I bet you were really knocked flat by that.'

'Yes—'

'Well, I'm fine and I'm having a whale of a time, so I hope you won't mind me not ringing again...' Her daughter's voice dropped very low before she continued, 'Sorry, but it looks really naff having to phone home.'

Seconds later, Daisy returned the phone to Alessio. He tossed it aside. A gulf of silence stretched and Daisy's brow furrowed when Alessio made no move to pull her back into his arms. Her still heated body tautened and flushed with guilty acknowledgement of her own lingering and intense arousal.

'I thought my memories might have been coloured by adolescent fantasy but they weren't.' His dark, deep voice flat with a curious lack of expression, Alessio cast her a sudden chillingly cold glance from below spiky black lashes, his brilliant dark gaze bleak and hard. Springing lithely off the bed, he reached for his shirt. 'You really *are* dynamite in bed ... but I think I'll take a rain check.'

Daisy's face flamed with shock and humiliation. That rejection slashed like a winter wind across her exposed flesh. She tugged the sheet over herself, her fingers bone-white as she clenched them beneath its cover. 'What's the matter with you?' she heard herself whisper strickenly.

Alessio swung back to her, his dramatically handsome features taut. His wide, sensual mouth twisted. 'I'm still very angry with you. Every time I remember that you took my daughter away from me, it makes me want to smash things. But I'll get over that. It's irrational to expect more from you than you are capable of giving and it's impossible to turn the clock back.'

Ill-prepared for that level of frankness, Daisy flinched. He had hidden that anger so well from her that she had been fooled. Now, when her every defence was down he condemned her with that reminder, throwing her into guilty confusion. 'You're not being fair.'

Alessio's screened gaze closed in on her and lingered in cool appraisal, his detachment somehow making her even more painfully aware of her nudity beneath the sheet. 'On the contrary, I am being very fair. You're a remarkably good mother. You're gorgeous and sexy and great in bed.'

Daisy bent her head, burning pink invading her cheeks afresh. But not so sexy and not so great that he couldn't still walk away, she thought, in an agony of mortification and self-loathing.

'That you should also be a little greedy and emotionally shallow is no big deal,' Alessio added grimly.

Her head flew up. 'I am not greedy... and I am not shallow!'

'Daisy, you have the staying power of a butterfly.'

'That's not true!'

'It's not important.' In the thundering silence, Alessio shrugged with an air of arrogant finality. 'If it wasn't for Tara, we wouldn't be here now.'

'I don't need you to tell me that.' He was only confirming what she had already known, what she had inexplicably allowed herself to forget over the past half-hour. Yet the reminder made Daisy feel incredibly empty and degraded. The intimacy she had foolishly believed they had recaptured had only been an illusion, born of her own stupid sentimentality and sexual hunger. She hated herself for that weakness. She wanted to lie down and die, but not in front of *him*.

Without warning, Alessio strode over to the door and flung it wide, an impatient frown drawing his black brows together. 'I think we have a visitor.'

'A visitor?' Daisy repeated in bewilderment.

A female voice echoed through the upper reaches of the villa, the distant tap-tap of stiletto heels sounding on the marble staircase, telegraphing their wearer's impatience.

'Bianca,' Alessio breathed, already moving out into the corridor to intercept his sister.

Daisy paled. 'But how on earth did she get in?' she gasped. 'Through a window on a broomstick?'

Alessio froze, his dark head whipping round, the smooth planes of his strong profile hardened by a flash of angry incredulity.

Daisy turned crimson as she realised what she had said.

'Grow up, Daisy,' Alessio advised with withering bite. 'You may be stuck in a time-warp but the rest of us have moved on. If you can't behave like an adult and be civil, I suggest that you stay up here!'

'I—'

But the door closed with a final thud. With a groan of frustration, Daisy flung herself back against the pillows. Smart move, Daisy. Alienate him more by attacking his twin. Alessio had no idea how much abuse she had once had to take from his sister. Daisy hadn't told tales. And it was too late now to redress the balance. She would only sound like a sulky child harbouring a grudge. And really Bianca was the least of her problems, she told herself painfully as she threw back the sheet and got up.

For only now did she truly appreciate the depth of Alessio's bitterness. In angry impatience, he had taken her beliefs and shaken them inside out, shattering her view of the past. Alessio had not been grateful to be released from their shotgun marriage. Alessio had been equally devastated by their divorce. He had actually thought *he* was the one being dumped.

That picture dredged a shaky laugh from Daisy but it also made her think. Bianca's assurance all those years ago that within months of their wedding her brother was already involved with his former girlfriend again no longer seemed credible. Had her sister-in-law lied about Sophia and that supposed reconciliation in a cruelly clever play on Daisy's insecurity?

Whatever—Daisy gave her head an impatient shake—naturally Alessio was still seething at the fact that after walking out on their marriage she had chosen to deny him all knowledge of his daughter. Alessio thought she was a greedy, shallow woman who could not be trusted. Although, with cool Leopardi calculation, he had not shared that news with her until *after* the wedding. Daisy shivered, suddenly cold with apprehension about what the future might hold. She had still fallen into his arms, her every defence destroyed, a physical hunger that terrified her betraying her with humiliating ease.

Ten minutes later, she descended the sweeping staircase, her battered confidence bolstered by the elegant pale blue dress she wore. Inside she was still a mess of see-sawing emotions and conflict but she had no intention of entertaining Bianca with a miserable face.

The front doors in the hall were wide open. On the last step of the stairs, Daisy froze. Alessio was standing outside with a blonde draped round him. Daisy blinked and looked again, unable to credit the evidence of her own eyes. Slender brown arms were linked round Alessio's throat as the woman laughed up at him, her flawless profile and the flowing mane of her corn-gold hair instantly recognisable to Daisy...

Her heart gave a sickening lurch as she was plunged into shock. Nina Franklin. What was *she* doing here? And why had Alessio led her to believe that the visitor was his sister? A stifled moan of distress trapped in her throat, Daisy reeled off the stairs before she could be seen and fled into the drawing room.

CHAPTER EIGHT

'SOMEHOW you don't look quite as smug as I expected,' a languidly amused female voice remarked.

Startled, Daisy spun round, breathless and bewildered. In shock, she focused on Alessio's sister. Bianca was standing by the window, a tall, rake-thin brunette in an enviably simple white shift-dress that screeched its designer cut. 'Bianca...?' she muttered dazedly, her brain refusing to function.

The only image stamped inside her head was that of Nina with her arms linked round Alessio, laughing and smiling with confident intimacy, certainly not reacting as any woman might have been expected to react when her lover had broken off their relationship and almost immediately married another woman. That disturbing image still twisted like a fiendish knife in Daisy's shrinking flesh.

Bianca strolled forward, a mocking smile pinned to her lips. 'Yes, I have to admit that much as I despise you, Daisy, I also have to admire your sheer nerve. You are holding a real live Leopardi as a hostage to fortune.'

In an uncertain gesture, Daisy pushed back damp tendrils of silver-fair hair from her brow. 'I don't know what you're talking about.'

'Tara...your miracle ticket back into the family circle!' Bianca vented a scornful laugh. 'But I wouldn't get too comfortable if I were you. Alessio may have married you to get custody of his daughter but I don't think he's planning to hang on to *both* of you—'

'What are you trying to say?' Daisy cut in tautly, fighting to get a grip on her wits again.

'So you *still* need everything spelt out in words of one syllable.' Bianca shot her a look of pitying superiority. 'Alessio will keep Tara and ditch you. And why not? The way he sees it, you did the same thing to him!'

'Why do you still hate me so much?' Daisy whispered in a shaken undertone, appalled by the brunette's continuing malice. 'And what on earth are you doing here?'

'You loused up my brother's life once and now you're trying to do it again. Twins stick together,' Bianca told her succinctly. 'As to what I'm doing here at the villa...business, strictly business, although I do feel that I ought to apologise for inadvertently reuniting Alessio with Nina. You're such a passionately jealous little soul, and what hope have you got against a girl that age?'

Daisy turned bone-white. 'You bitch,' she mumbled strickenly.

'*Madre di Dio*, what the devil is going on here?' Alessio's whiplike intervention cut across the room like an icy wind on a hot summer day.

Sharply disconcerted, Daisy whirled round, cannoned into an occasional table and sent an exquisite vase of flowers smashing down onto the marble hearth of the fireplace. Glass flew everywhere. 'Oh, *hell*!' she gasped, and automatically dropped down, intending to gather up the shattered shards of crystal.

Bianca released her breath in a long-suffering hiss. 'I'm afraid that your wife is not prepared to let bygones be bygones, Alessio. I tried...now you can't say I didn't try...but you heard what she called me, didn't you?'

'Daisy, *leave* that glass alone!' Dark eyes blazing, the cast of his strong features implacable, Alessio followed up the scorching command by striding over and hauling

Daisy upright. 'Right now we can do without a blood-spattered bride playing a starring role here.'

'It must be a frightful embarrassment to be so clumsy,' Bianca commented drily.

As her teeth sank into the soft underside of her lower lip and absolutely brutalised the tender flesh, Daisy tasted the sharp, acrid tang of blood in her mouth. Bianca had heard Alessio's approach, she realised, and all Alessio had heard was Daisy insulting his sister.

'I'm sorry Daisy has been so rude,' Alessio drawled with gritty delivery, one powerful hand anchored to his wife's slight shoulder like an imprisoning chain, long brown fingers exerting meaningful pressure. 'But I'm sure that she wants to apologise for losing her temper.'

Daisy went rigid and remained mute, outraged to be dragged forward like a misbehaving child and ordered to eat humble pie. Frustration and fury lanced through her, for she was painfully aware that anything she said now in her own defence would not be convincing.

'Don't worry about it,' Bianca sighed with a forgiving smile.

Daisy surveyed the brunette with barely concealed loathing, every nerve in her body still jangling from what she had both witnessed and withstood in the space of ten nightmare minutes.

'Under the circumstances...' Alessio hesitated, and then shrugged a fatalistic shoulder. 'You *can* use the grounds for your fashion shoot. I appreciate that it would be difficult to find another venue at such short notice—'

'I knew Nina would change your mind!' Bianca carolled in a nauseating tone of girlish relief.

Daisy's teeth ground together.

'We only need a few hours and the crew are already here,' Bianca continued sweetly and apologetically. 'I know it's very inconvenient timing but I never dreamt that you and Daisy might be coming to this old place for your honeymoon!'

In a sudden movement that took Alessio by surprise, Daisy tore herself free of his restraining hand and stalked out of the room.

'*Dio...*' Bianca groaned in her wake. 'If I'd known it was likely to cause this much trouble for you, I'd never have asked!'

Daisy raced up the stairs like a woman jet-propelled. Not one more moment would she spend in this house, not *one* more moment...not for Tara, not for anybody! She was getting out right now! Her breath catching in sobs in her throat, she trailed her still unpacked suitcase across the dressing-room floor and struggled to close it, stuffing in sleeves and protruding hems of clothing disarranged in her haste to get dressed only minutes earlier.

'What the hell do you think you're playing at now?' Alessio enquired from the doorway.

Daisy jerked round on her knees, two spots of enraged colour burning over her cheekbones. 'Get out of my way, you swine! No, you're not a swine, you're lower than that! You're a snake—a sneaky, sly, double-dealing, *stupid* snake...because if you think I intend to stay here and put up with you, your girlfriend and your shrew of a sister you're living in fantasy land!'

Alessio folded his arms and stood his ground. 'You're not going anywhere, *piccola mia*,' he spelt out rawly.

'Do you think that treating me like a child means you can ground me like one?' Daisy launched back, angrier than she had ever been in her life, her eyes burning an incandescent violet challenge.

'I think that if I strip you naked, trash all your clothes and keep you locked in the bedroom you'll find it a little difficult to stray beyond these walls.'

'You wouldn't *dare*!' Daisy told him, flying furiously upright.

'Try me,' Alessio invited with soft menace, his shimmering eyes striking threatening sparks off her incredulous stare. 'When my daughter's happiness is at risk, I don't think there is anything that I wouldn't dare.'

'What's that supposed to mean?'

'It means that the day you walk out on this marriage I start fighting to keep Tara in Italy with me. I will not be shut out of her life again,' Alessio asserted with harsh emphasis.

Daisy went white with shock, a shiver of cold fear slithering down her rigid spine. That uncompromising threat electrified her. All of a sudden, Bianca's spiteful allegations no longer seemed quite so fanciful. Alessio was already letting her know that if their marriage failed he would fight to retain custody of their daughter. Was it at all possible that he might also be planning to use Daisy for as long as he needed her to get Tara settled in... before dispensing with her services as a wife and mother altogether? Or was that a paranoid suspicion?

'You are scaring me,' Daisy muttered in a surge of involuntary candour.

'Maybe you scare *me* when you haul out a suitcase barely twenty-four hours after you say "I do" for the second time!' Alessio was very pale beneath his golden skin but fierce determination harshly delineated his sculpted bone structure. 'Now, I don't expect you to become bosom pals with my sister but I do expect a mature acceptance that my family are also Tara's family and that when she arrives here at the end of the week she does not need to be dragged into the midst of some continuing, petty war that started before she was even born!'

'I did not restart the war.'

Alessio spread his lean, strong hands in a bold arc of impatience with a subject he clearly considered beneath his notice. 'I will not allow Tara to come home to us for the first time and find a hostile atmosphere—'

'And what are you intending to do to improve that atmosphere?' A laugh that was no laugh at all escaped Daisy as she recalled the humiliation of his earlier rejection. Fighting blindly to conserve her pride, torn with savage pain and confusion, she thrust up her chin in defiance. 'I hate you, Alessio. I *really* hate you for what you've done to me today!'

'Or maybe you hate me for what I didn't do!' Throwing her off balance, Alessio cast an explicit and suggestive glance back towards the disordered bed. Bold eyes flaming over her, he murmured thickly, 'I can hardly believe now that I walked away from temptation.'

Affected more than she could bear by that mercurial change of mood and direction, her breasts rising and falling with the accelerated pace of her breathing, Daisy said with hoarse emphasis, 'You'll get your face slapped if you try to walk back again!'

'When did that prospect ever inhibit me?' Alessio flashed her a look of sudden vibrant amusement. 'You ought to know by now that I relish a challenge.'

Without the smallest warning, Daisy's heart turned a somersault and her mouth went dry.

A wolfish smile curved Alessio's mobile mouth. 'But you can relax. You're safe for the moment. The staff are waiting to serve lunch.'

'Lunch?' Daisy echoed foolishly.

With difficulty, she tore her gaze from the intense lure of those entrapping golden eyes. All over again she was devastated by her inability to control or suppress her powerful sexual response to him.

'Our unwelcome guests will be busy in the grounds. We'll be alone,' Alessio pointed out soothingly.

'Unwelcome?' Daisy queried tautly, uncertainly.

'*Dio* ... surely you don't imagine that I wanted this three-act circus descending on us?' Alessio's mouth twisted with expressive incredulity. 'But they'll be gone soon enough.'

'Why did Bianca need your permission to use the grounds?' Daisy prompted on the way downstairs, her outrage at the situation ebbing a little as she appreciated that Alessio was no more pleased by the invasion than she was.

'I own the villa now. When Vittorio decided to sell, I bought.'

'So what has your sister got to do with a fashion shoot?'

'Three months ago she became the owner of a photographic studio. She's trying very hard to make a mark on the fashion world. Nina's a top model,' Alessio explained. 'Bianca needs her star quality to sell this layout and as Nina is a friend of the family she agreed to help.'

Daisy reconsidered the view she had had of Nina and Alessio together, belatedly conceding that she had seen nothing that might not be described as an affectionate greeting. 'Nina ... is a family friend?'

'Our parents move in the same social circles.'

'I saw you with her,' Daisy heard herself admit with shocking abruptness. 'She was all over you like chickenpox!'

Alessio shifted a broad shoulder beneath Daisy's piercing sideways scrutiny. 'Nina is very demonstrative. Showbiz-type personalities usually are. And, to be frank, *cara*, she's behaving generously. I *was* seeing her up until very recently.' He delivered the reminder with a hint of reproof.

Horrified to be riven with a white-hot streak of jealousy, Daisy found herself surveying her meal with little appetite. Just knowing that the beautiful, *generous* Nina was around made her feel deeply insecure. Only this morning she had been telling herself that she could handle a marriage of convenience, but already she was drowning in an emotional morass of pain and confusion. Why was it that no other man had ever had the power to tear at her heart with one teasing smile and stop it beating altogether by the simple act of donning a pair of jeans?

Having dismissed the staff, Alessio replenished her wine with his own hand. Daisy watched those long, lean, denim-clad legs advancing and momentarily shut her eyes in despair, because every treacherous pulse in her body was pounding insanely fast.

'You're not eating,' Alessio commented tautly.

'Maybe what I want isn't on the plate,' Daisy said wildly, loathing herself for her own bodily weakness. She was turning into a sex-starved animal but she would leave him, stark naked if necessary, before she allowed him to find that out!

'Just tell me what you want and I'll order it for you.'

Daisy gave an agonised little quiver, her imagination leaving her suspended between heaven and hell. 'I'm not hungry—'

'You haven't eaten since last night!' Alessio grated. 'Do you have a problem with food?'

'What is this *thing* you have about my eating habits?'

Alessio shot her a look of exasperation 'I knew a girl with anorexia nervosa at university. Sophia...Sophia Corsini, now, she—'

That particular name did grab Daisy's full attention. 'Your girlfriend was anorexic?' she cut in sharply.

'Sophia was in most of my classes but I never dated her,' Alessio countered with a faint frown of distaste and surprise at the suggestion. 'She was one very mixed-up kid. She dropped out in the middle of our second year.'

Her eyes lowering from his, Daisy mulled over that calm explanation. She believed him. Colour rose slowly in her cheeks. Bianca had made up a story and Daisy had foolishly swallowed it without demanding evidence or confronting Alessio. Clearly, there had been no other girl involved in the breakup of their first marriage. And yet hadn't she been ready to give credence to Bianca's spiteful allegations a *second* time? Should she tell Alessio what had really happened with his sister? Would he believe her? she wondered ruefully. Bianca was a very overprotective and possessive twin, but clever enough to hide it. Daisy was almost certain that she had been treated to a side of Bianca that Alessio had yet to experience.

'What are you thinking about?' Alessio probed, taking in her evasive gaze and guilty flush.

'You actually thought I might be anorexic too?' Lifting up her head, eager to move the subject in a safer direction, Daisy studied him, and an undeniable lurch of tenderness warmed her. He had been worried about her, concerned about her health. She picked up her knife and fork. 'Tense situations kill my appetite,' she told him. 'That's all.'

'But that wasn't what you were thinking about,' Alessio said perceptively, after watching her clear her plate in careful silence.

'Maybe I was thinking about just how well I know you...in fact, how well I *ever* knew you,' Daisy said unsteadily.

'I'm a very average guy,' Alessio asserted lazily, his lush black lashes partially screening eyes of vibrant gold which interfered with her ability to breathe.

'You think so?' Daisy responded a little unevenly, struggling to close out the flash-fire effect of those gorgeous eyes. 'You know...I need fresh air more than I need caffeine. It's very airless in here.'

But Alessio sprang up and caught her as she left the table, tugging her up against him with hard, insistent hands, every muscle in his big, powerful body tense as he stared down at her with unhidden frustration. 'We're married now. Don't shut me out...and don't run away from me.'

The hard masculine thrust of his virility against her taut stomach made her slender length hum and throb like a race car revving up. A bitter-sweet ache made her thighs clench, leaving her dizzy and disorientated. But even as her hips began to rise in a tiny, inviting circular motion as old as time, and the kind of fierce, unquenchable longing that burned engulfed her, Daisy fought her own frailty with frantic determination.

'We're making a home for Tara. That's all we're doing,' she told him unsteadily. 'Now...*please* let go of me!'

His smouldering gaze told her that he wasn't about to listen and then a door slammed, voices intruding from the hall, and Alessio released her with a raw expletive. On legs that felt as reliable as cotton-wool sticks, Daisy fled through the French windows. But she felt as though she had left half of herself behind in the broken circle of his arms. A stifled sob tore at her throat, her eyes smarting with stinging tears as she breathed in the hot, still air and saw right to the very heart of her turmoil.

Only loving had ever hurt this much. Alessio influenced her every emotion and response. And that was so achingly, terrifyingly familiar to Daisy. She could have coped so much better with being a sex-starved animal. The idea that she might still *love* Alessio petrified her. Loving him meant that the very last thing she could live with was a humiliating marriage of convenience cobbled together solely for their daughter's sake.

Indeed, much as she loved Tara, if Alessio told her once more that they were only married again for *her* benefit she would scream and push him out of a window, because every time he stressed the all-encompassing importance of Tara's needs it made Daisy feel as if she herself was of no account. And why was she so pathetically envious of his affection for her daughter? Because she wanted more for herself. In short, she was still hopelessly in love with the same male who had stolen her heart at seventeen. Why had it taken her this long to work that out?

In a daze of conflicting emotions, Daisy watched Alessio stride down the steps at the front of the villa, a devastatingly handsome male whose every lithe, graceful movement made her shockingly aware not only of him but also of her own extreme vulnerability. Hurriedly, she looked away again, only then giving some attention to the scene before her. Nina was posing in a gorgeous shoulderless sugar-pink evening dress against the dark yew topiary. Tara had once had a Barbie doll that looked remarkably similar. Impossibly perfect, dressed like a fairy-tale princess, complete with a cloud of golden hair.

Bianca drifted over. 'Stunning, isn't she?'

Daisy was watching Nina blowing a flirtatious kiss at Alessio between takes. 'I don't believe in the coincidence of you *and* Nina arriving today—'

'But Alessio does. Obviously I knew you were staying here,' Bianca confirmed drily.

Irritably brushing off the attentions of the fluttering make-up girl, Nina approached Alessio with the efficiency of a heat-seeking missile closing in on a target.

'You're a week too late,' Daisy told Bianca firmly. 'You should have tried this charade *before* the wedding!'

'I'm merely bringing a continuing relationship to your attention,' Bianca responded sweetly. 'Does Nina strike you as a woman who has recently lost her lover to a wife? She knows why Alessio married you and she knows it won't last long. She can afford to be understanding.'

Nina had engaged Alessio in animated conversation. Daisy tilted her chin and walked over. Nina ignored her. Alessio settled a casual, long-fingered hand on the base of her spine. Daisy leant against him in a sudden tiny but aggressive movement and dug her fingers into the back pocket of his jeans, her seemingly idle fingernails scoring the flexing muscles of his lean hip. The scent and the heat of him engulfed her. An infinitesimal quiver ran through her. A seductress well on the way to becoming a hopeless victim of her own ploy, Daisy sucked in oxygen in a despairing rush, feeling Alessio tense and shift, while she dazedly questioned the inconsistency of her provocative behaviour.

'Let's go for a walk,' Alessio breathed with telling abruptness.

Nina opened her green eyes wide. 'But I can't. I have to get into my next outfit in five minutes.' She frowned down at Daisy, too self-centred even to realise that the invitation had not been directed at her. 'Oh, yes, I almost forgot. Barry gave me a message for you.'

'Barry?' Daisy frowned, momentarily thrown by the reference.

'I went to view that house with him,' Nina said carelessly. 'I felt really sorry for him too. He's terribly broken up about losing you.'

Before Daisy could part her lips to challenge that astonishing assurance, Alessio intervened curtly, 'And the message?'

Nina looked coy. 'He said to remind Daisy of the proposition he made the night before your wedding.

'Barry wants you to give him the chance to manage the agency,' Daisy proffered beneath Alessio's chillingly unimpressed gaze while Nina walked back to the cameras wearing a feline smile of satisfaction. 'He's very ambitious. Why are you looking at me like that?'

Alessio shook free of her.

Daisy's lashes fluttered and she groaned, 'Oh, no, you're still a jealous toad!'

His eyes blazed with derision, his mouth twisting. 'You have to be out of your mind to think that,' he drawled with icy precision.

Yes, possibly she was...for wasn't she attributing emotions to him that he did not possess? There had to be some degree of caring for jealousy to exist. And Alessio did not care. Alessio's sole concern was Tara. Flushing a hot, mortified pink, Daisy spun away and headed off for the cover of the trees, feeling that she'd made an outsize ass of herself. Let Bianca and Nina play out their stupid farce, she decided ruefully. They would be gone soon enough.

How *could* she have hidden from what was in her own heart when she'd married Alessio again? Her emotions had threatened to tear her in two with their contrary promptings. Yet still she had refused to see them for what they were. She still loved Alessio. What price their marriage of convenience now? And in forcing her into that agreement hadn't Alessio really been giving her what she secretly wanted? She burned with shame at that acknowledgement.

Curled up in the shade of the giant oaks on the edge of the estate, she found herself inexorably reliving powerful and disturbing memories of the teenagers they had once been, so intensely and exclusively involved in each other that they had always wanted to be alone. Could she possibly settle for less now? Could she live with a man who only needed her to keep his daughter happy? In such an empty relationship, it would kill her by degrees to be a real wife to Alessio, she conceded painfully.

'Do you realise what time it is?'

Daisy paused halfway up the stairs and studiously consulted her watch. 'Half past nine.'

His lean features a set mask of self-restraint, Alessio nonetheless prowled like a sleek, dark, hungry predator across the hall and spread his hands expressively. 'Where the hell have you been until this hour?' he gritted from between clenched teeth.

'I went for a walk. I thought I'd give our visitors a chance to get on their bikes,' Daisy said tightly. 'Sorry I missed out on dinner but I made myself a sandwich in the kitchen. Now I'm off to bed. Goodnight.'

'*Goodnight?*' Alessio raked, the mask slipping slightly to allow her a view of the angry exasperation he was struggling to control.

Daisy hurried into the dressing room off their bedroom. Frustratingly, her case had been unpacked while she had been out. After locating a nightdress, Daisy removed herself again at speed and selected a small bedroom on the second floor. Only when she had got into bed and doused the light did she begin to relax a little. Alessio would get the message eventually. They could be . . . well, parenting partners. Anything more intimate was out of the question and as long as she kept her feelings to herself, as long as he had no suspicion of his power over her he couldn't hurt her again, could he?

Some time later, a distant dull thud broke the silence of the villa. Daisy frowned when within the space of a minute another thud followed . . . and then another. She lost count but realised in growing horror that the racket of slamming doors was getting louder and closer, not to mention more intimidating, by the second. The image of Alessio striding through the villa conducting something as uncool as a room-to-room search for his missing bride shook her rigid but Daisy stayed where she was, as stiff and tense as a sacrificial offering, until finally and with an almighty crash that matched her heartbeat the door flew wide.

'I ought to chain you to a wall in the cellar!' Alessio launched at her in a roar of raw derision as he strode over to the bed and stared fulminatingly down at her shrinking figure. 'At least then I'd know where to find you! You spend half the damned day hiding in the woods and then creep up here to the attics to spend the night. What sort of a marriage do you call this?'

'This is not a normal marriage—'

'But it's about to become one!' Alessio swore with conviction as he dragged back the bedding and hauled her up into his arms before she could even draw breath to evade him.

'Put me down!' Daisy screeched in shock, having been prepared for argument but not physical intervention.

'You're supposed to be in my bedroom. That's where you're going. And if you don't want to sleep in the bed with me you can sleep on the floor... but one thing I do know—you are sleeping in the same room. Why? Because you are my *wife!*' Alessio spelt out with wrathful emphasis.

'You blackmailed me into becoming your wife!'

'Come off it,' Alessio countered with blistering contempt, thundering down the stairs two at a time and striding along the corridor. 'On your terms the blackmail was manna from heaven!'

'I... beg... your... pardon?' Daisy gasped, devastated that he should already be harbouring such a suspicion.

'You want me every bit as much as I want you... and only this way could you have me without admitting that fact. Manna from heaven!' Alessio repeated with provocative bite as he dumped her down on the bed.

'That's an absolutely ridiculous accusation!' Daisy struggled to sound convincingly incredulous but she had turned scarlet.

'And since nothing will convince me that you don't want me... mutual lust being instantly recognisable... I can't understand why you're still running in the wrong direction!' Alessio delivered with savage candour. 'What more do you want from me? What does it take for me to get some co-operation? Do I need to tell you that there is a string of credit cards and a monthly allowance that would keep an oil sheikh happy waiting for you?'

Daisy paled and swallowed hard at the degrading suggestion that money might make her more amenable. Suddenly, playing the role of gold-digger who had gone out with a big unfeeling bang during their first marriage no longer felt like a source of secret amusement or a clever defence mechanism. Maybe it was time she told Alessio the truth about that financial settlement. She worried at her lower lip, feeling threatened by the prospect of even telling Alessio that much. But how could it hurt? At least he wouldn't be able to call her mercenary again!

'And the sound of your silence will not get us anywhere fast!' Alessio bit out.

Daisy cleared her throat awkwardly but Alessio had already vanished into the bathroom. In an abrupt movement, she yanked up two pillows and placed them carefully in a defensive line down the centre of the bed.

Alessio hit the mattress and the barrier simultaneously. He sat up again and vented an expletive in Italian. 'Sometimes you are so bloody childish...'

'It is not childish of me to believe that our relationship will work best if we sleep apart,' Daisy protested shakily. 'And, by the way, I am not greedy and grasping and I never was!'

An expectant hush fell.

'Is that the end of this astonishing rush of confidence?' Alessio probed drily.

Colouring with annoyance, Daisy breathed in deep and forced herself onward, telling herself that it would be very much to her advantage to embarrass him with the truth. She tilted her chin. 'Your father persuaded Janet to accept that settlement on my behalf. She put it in a

Swiss bank account and she didn't tell me it was there until last week.'

'*Madre di Dio...*' Alessio breathed in a shaken surge of comprehension, his deep voice fracturing. A split second later he attempted to breach the pillows but Daisy was ready for that eventuality.

She rolled out of bed and took up a defensive stance. 'So you can stop calling me greedy, and I don't need your credit cards or your lousy allowance because that settlement would keep Tara and me in comfort for the rest of our days!'

'You weren't lying when you said you didn't take a penny when you divorced me...' Spiky black lashes swept up to reveal shrewd, questioning eyes of gold as he surveyed her with intense interest and none of the embarrassment she had expected. 'So at what stage did you decide that you preferred me to think that you *were* greedy and grasping? What were you trying to cover up?'

Chagrined pink flooded Daisy's small face. The speed with which Alessio could assimilate new information and dissect it horrified her. 'I...I—'

'Then you genuinely did think that you were doing me a favour by divorcing me and keeping quiet about Tara,' Alessio reflected out loud. 'Daisy the martyr— now that does have a far more convincing ring of reality. You let my father bully you into the divorce, didn't you?' He drove a not quite steady hand through his luxuriant black hair and looked heavenwards, his strong jawline set fiercely hard.

The silence grew and lingered until her tension seemed to scream beneath its weight.

'Daisy...were you still in love with me when you divorced me?' Alessio enquired in a tone of the utmost casualness.

The silence was like the clash of cymbals in Daisy's ears. She was appalled. One little thing, just one little thing she had confessed, and within the space of a minute he was sprinting for the finishing line.

'Gosh, I'm so tired,' she mumbled round a fake yawn, desperate fingers splayed to conceal her hot, discomfited face.

'Come back to bed,' Alessio purred in husky invitation. 'I'll wake you up fast.'

Involuntarily, Daisy hovered, violet eyes wide, a vulnerable prey to the lure of him. She thought of his hands on her body and a shiver of raw excitement coursed through her. A hungry need that she could not withstand held her fast. Why not give him the chance to prove that *his* way could work? an insidious voice murmured in the back of her mind.

'I won't risk another pregnancy,' Alessio imparted with measured emphasis. 'Is that what is worrying you? I don't want another child.'

And instantly that voice in Daisy's mind was silenced. A curious pain stabbed through her in its wake. Surely more children should at least have been a possibility in the normal marriage which Alessio had said he wanted? Yet he'd cooly dismissed the idea of extending the family before it could even arise.

In an abrupt movement, her every suspicion as to his marital intentions reawakened, Daisy grabbed at the light quilt lying at the foot of the bed. Beneath Alessio's utterly incredulous gaze, she wrapped herself within its folds and curled up in a comfortable armchair.

she had made a first nervous step towards lowering her defences when she had told him about that night on the plane. She had to be strong with herself, she thought. She had the still distressing memory to be convinced that the loving contentment of her teenage dreams could be her escape should not be dangerous... family embrace.

CHAPTER NINE

IN DAISY'S dream, the most perfect baby in the world lay before her, unclaimed. She was in the very act of eagerly reaching out to take possession when a pair of cruel, unfeeling hands got there first. 'I said *no*.' Alessio's voice intervened in icy disapproval and the seductive vision of sweet-smelling, lovable baby vanished.

Daisy woke up with tears trapped in her throat. A maid was pulling back the curtains. She was in bed but she was alone. She had a hazy recollection of briefly, blissfully snuggling into masculine arms *and* of the moan of distress which had escaped her when she had been released all too quickly into the cool embrace of a sheet. Her cheeks reddened fiercely. How long would it be before Alessio appreciated that she ran in the wrong direction only because she couldn't trust herself too close? Or did he already appreciate that?

As for that stupid dream, she thought painfully, she hadn't realised just how much she would love another baby until Alessio had announced that there wasn't going to be one. She had experienced a deep sense of rejection. Her distrust and insecurity had taken over again. One unpleasant fact stared her in the face. If there *was* any truth in the suggestion that Alessio might be looking on their marriage as only a temporary expedient, a second child would definitely be on the forbidden list.

Even so, within twenty-four hours of remarriage, Alessio had still turned her every conviction inside out. Yesterday she had hidden behind her pride but last night she had made a first nervous step towards lowering her defences when she had told him about that Swiss bank account. She had to be honest with herself at least. She loved the rat. She desperately wanted to be convinced that their marriage *was* real and that it did have a future.

As her steps sounded on the stairs some twenty minutes later, Alessio strolled out of the drawing room. A shaft of sunlight glittered across his luxuriant black hair, burnished his eyes and threw into prominence his hard, classic cheekbones and beautiful mouth. Intense sexual awareness literally froze Daisy in her tracks. She couldn't take her eyes off him. She could barely breathe. Her heart pounded in her eardrums, the blades of unquenched desire scissoring cruelly through her taut length, filling her with embarrassing heat as every pulse raced.

Alessio threw back his head, hooded knowing eyes resting on her with a flicker of lazy amusement. 'I knew you would sleep late. You had an extremely restless night.'

Her face flamed.

'We're going out for lunch,' he drawled.

A Ferrari was parked on the gravel outside. There was something oddly, disturbingly familiar about the vehicle but Daisy wasn't capable of making a connection at that moment. She climbed in on shaking legs, scarcely conscious of what she was doing. A hunger that had no limit had possessed her, shattering her with its greedy intensity. She lifted a trembling hand to push back her hair, overtly conscious of the aching fullness of her breasts and the painful tautness of her nipples.

Soon after, in the thundering silence, Alessio brought the powerful car to a slow halt in a lay-by screened from the road by a thick line of trees. There was something

even more awesomely familiar about that view beyond
the windscreen. But still its significance escaped Daisy;
it merely confused her more. With a seemingly casual
hand Alessio reached out and released her seat belt. 'You
deserve to be in agony,' he murmured softly. 'You're a
stubborn little witch. You could try trusting me...'

'Trusting you?' Daisy was way beyond reasoning.

'If I can forgive you for Tara, you can forgive me for
being too bloody proud to follow you over to London.'

Her breath caught in her throat, her eyes widening.
In a handful of words Alessio had plunged right to the
heart of the divisions between them, found them equal
and dismissed them, almost...almost as if he had already
worked out that her distrust stemmed from the
tremendous pain she had endured when they had
separated.

Alessio leant over her, smouldering eyes holding her
entrapped. 'And this...this *now*—this is where we begin
again. You, me, nothing else.'

Like a programmed doll, Daisy raised a jerky hand
and slowly ran a helplessly caressing fingertip along the
sensual curve of his firm mouth. 'I loved you so much,'
she whispered, remembered distress fracturing her soft
voice.

'That makes *such* a difference, *piccola mia*.' A vibrant smile slashing his dark features, Alessio parted his
lips to capture that marauding finger and lave it with his
tongue.

Daisy moaned low in her throat, a fierce ache stirring
between her thighs and turning her boneless. Her eyelids
lowered on passion-glazed eyes, her back arcing as she
slid languorously lower in the seat. Her submissive response dragged a stifled groan from Alessio. He eased
a hand beneath the hem of her dress, exploring the

smooth skin of her inner thigh. Her legs slid softly apart. The mere stroke of a finger against the burning heat and moisture beneath her silky panties reduced her to whimpering, quivering subjection.

'This was supposed to be your punishment, not mine,' Alessio confessed thickly.

Daisy's gaze ran down the poised length of his powerful body to the throbbing hardness outlined by the tight fit of his jeans and she melted simultaneously. 'Go home?' she framed in a shaky, choky suggestion.

Alessio thrust a hungry hand into the fall of her hair and stabbed her lips apart in a raw, forceful kiss of sexual frustration. But then he pulled back from her and reinstated her seat belt, cursing under his breath when it proved recalcitrant. In complete bemusement, Daisy struggled to focus on him as he started up the Ferrari again.

'We're lunching with my parents,' Alessio proffered in taut explanation.

'Oh...' Daisy said simply, too much in the grip of other impressions and responses to react. Finally she was making that bewildering connection. 'This is the same car you used to take me out in and we used to stop here before you dropped me back at the Morgans'.'

'*Dio*, Daisy... have you only just worked that out?'

The *same* car, she though dazedly. He had kept the Ferrari all these years. Alessio wasn't sentimental. Yet he had also brought her back to the villa, to the same bedroom, the same bed... His own daughter had called him madly romantic and impetuous. Oh, dear heaven, Daisy reflected, seriously shaken by that novel idea. How blind could a woman be? Was it possible that Alessio was as obsessively set on recapturing what they had lost as she herself was?

'My parents are flying over to London in a couple of days, ostensibly to view houses...but really to lie in wait for their one and only grandchild from France. It would be a very nice gesture if you were to agree to them flying her back here,' Alessio murmured.

'No problem,' Daisy mumbled dizzily.

And astonishingly there wasn't. Daisy drifted into the imposing Roman mansion which had provided the backdrop for the most miserable, tension-filled weeks of her life and met not the Borgias in twentieth-century guise but two older people clearly under strain but as anxious to mend fences as she was.

'We didn't welcome you into the family as we should have done the first time you were married,' Vittorio admitted with rueful emphasis, his eyes meeting Daisy's levelly. 'We were still looking for someone to blame. And unfortunately watching the two of you together then was like watching two cars with blindfolded drivers racing towards a pile-up. Alessio seemed to suffer a personality change overnight. You weren't any happier. I engineered the divorce in the honest belief that I was doing what had to be done.'

Registering his sincerity, Daisy swallowed hard and nodded.

'But you still didn't tell me the truth about that settlement,' Alessio reminded his father grimly.

Vittorio Leopardi grimaced and sighed. 'At the time it seemed best to leave it buried.'

Alessio's mother cleared her throat and murmured with unhidden eagerness, 'I expect you'll want to have more children as soon as possible...'

Daisy tensed, her eyes flying to Alessio.

'I shouldn't think so,' he said, directing a quelling glance at his parent.

Daisy lowered her head. Stupid to feel rejected, she told herself. Even more stupid to feel suspicious of his motives. How could she blame him for feeling like that? Alessio could have only the most disastrous memories of her last pregnancy. But, whatever lay behind his reasoning, it still hurt, she acknowledged.

Alessio reached for her hand as they walked back out into the sunlight. 'You see... the monsters were in your imagination. My parents are well aware of how badly they behaved in the past.'

His understanding touched something deep inside Daisy. She met his golden gaze and her heart skipped a beat, her pulses pounding. Concentration became impossible. They didn't talk much on the drive back. Having narrowly missed a ticket for speeding, Alessio shot the Ferrari through the gates of the villa with a groan of relief.

'Do you remember what we did to recover from your very first meeting with my family?' he murmured thickly.

Daisy went hot all over and blushed. It had taken too many glasses of wine to carry her through that long-ago meal with the coldly disapproving Leopardis. Alessio had carried her up the stairs, laughingly asserting that he couldn't take her home until she had sobered up, and... she had tried to take his jeans off with her teeth.

'I'm still waiting for you to do that again.'

'You didn't wait then,' Daisy muttered, alarmingly short of breath.

'Practice makes perfect,' Alessio breathed in a husky, sensual growl.

They were crossing the hall in a direct line to the stairs when a maid appeared. 'There is a Signor Barry Stevens on the phone, *signora*,' she recited breathlessly.

'B-Barry?' Daisy stammered in surprise.

'How the hell did *he* get this number?' Alessio launched down at her accusingly.

'I don't know!'

His hard mouth twisted, his brilliant eyes suddenly icy cold. 'Obviously you've been in contact with him since we arrived.'

Daisy swept up the phone in the library. 'Who gave you this number?' she hissed down the line without any preliminaries.

'It was waiting for me when I got back to the office yesterday. I understand that you wanted me to call!'

'No,' Daisy groaned.

'So you don't have any news for me?' he pressed thinly. 'Then who left that flipping message telling me to contact you?'

'I'm afraid it must have been someone's idea of a joke. Barry...please don't call here again,' Daisy sighed wearily.

Alessio was still standing in the hall, his dark, strong face impassive and set like granite.

Daisy snatched in a deep breath. 'Alessio...either Bianca or Nina must be responsible for giving Barry this number because I have not been in touch with him—'

'Why the hell would either of them want to do something like that?'

'Both of them seem equally keen to cause trouble between us,' Daisy stated doggedly, her chin coming up in response to his blatant incredulity.

'I'm not into crazy conspiracy theories, Daisy. If your toy boy is missing you, find someone else to blame. But don't insult my intelligence by trying to drag my sister or Nina into the mess you've left in your wake!'

The acrid sting of tears struck Daisy's strained eyes. 'You said...you said that I could try trusting you...when are *you* going to try trusting *me*? she prompted painfully.

Alessio dealt her a look of bleak contempt and strode out of the house.

Daisy folded her arms in a jerky motion and then her patience snapped. What a moody, volatile swine Alessio could still be! No matter what he said, he was still as suspicious as hell of her every move.

Desperately keen to look as if she had barely noticed his absence, Daisy was floating on a Lilo in the swimming pool when Alessio put in a reappearance. Since it had taken so much effort to get onto the Lilo, she didn't twitch a muscle behind her sunglasses and maintained an attitude of sun-worshipping relaxation and cool.

'If you've got into that water without learning how to swim, I'll kill you!' Alessio spelt out in a raw opening salvo.

Daisy looked smug. 'I can swim...I can even life-save.'

'Since when?'

'Since I found an instructor who didn't think dropping me in the deep end and telling me I would float would miraculously do the trick.'

'Come out,' Alessio ordered.

'Why should I?' Daisy retorted, sitting up suddenly and without due care and attention. The Lilo lurched and she made a frantic attempt to correct her balance but still ended up being tipped into the water with a gigantic splash.

'Stop it...*let go*!' she spluttered when she found herself being towed back to the side, incredulous that Alessio had dived into the water in a quite ludicrous rescue bid fully clothed. 'I *told* you that I could swim!'

Alessio dragged her back up the steps regardless. 'I'd like to see some proof of your proficiency before I risk standing around while you drown.'

Infuriated by her inability to strike an impressive note of injured dignity around Alessio, Daisy snatched up a towel to dry her face, pushing her tangled hair out of her eyes with furious hands. 'You make me so mad sometimes, I could scream!'

' "O lady, speak again!" ' Alessio quoted with deep irony.

It took a second or two for Daisy to absorb the shock of Alessio throwing lines of Shakespeare at her. *'Romeo and Juliet?'* she scorned with a curled lip. 'I don't think so. And I am not playing Desdemona to your Othello!'

'It would indeed be difficult.' Alessio elevated a winged brow sardonically. 'Desdemona didn't have a past that encompassed half the men in the UK.'

'How dare you?' Daisy gasped in outrage.

In thunderous silence, Alessio peeled off his sodden jeans and shirt, his rough, impatient movements lacking his usual grace and cool. Mesmerised against her will, Daisy watched him execute a perfect dive and plough in a fast, aggressive crawl through the water.

Walking to the edge, Daisy waited for him to hit the side and crouched down in readiness. 'You think I made love with every one of them, don't you?'

Stormy golden eyes struck hers like forked lightning. 'What do you think?' Alessio bit back with slashing derision, and launched into another deeply aggressive length of the pool.

The next time he touched base, Daisy murmured, 'Alessio...?'

'I don't want to know,' he grated, and, planting his hands on the tiled edge, he hauled himself up, water streaming from his lean, powerfully muscled body in rivulets that glistened on his bronzed skin. Watching him, Daisy found it extraordinarily hard to recall what she had been about to say. Inflating her lungs again was even more of a challenge. He strode past her stark naked and stood towel-drying his hair.

'Put your eyes back in your head and look the other way like a lady, Daisy,' Alessio advised silkily with his back turned to her.

A deep crimson flooded her cheeks. 'I—'

'I can *feel* you looking at me. I always could.'

'It's a little hard to ignore a naked man.'

'Is it? Do you recall that nudist beach I once took you to? You welded shut your eyes and hung onto your bikini like it was the only thing that stood between you and moral damnation!'

'That must have given you a laugh.'

'Actually... it shamed me into taking you home.'

'About those albums—'

'*Piccola mia*, you are not as a rule this persistent. I have no desire to talk about your rogues' gallery of photographic trophies.'

'I haven't had a single serious relationship since our divorce!' Daisy admitted grudgingly.

'Tell me something that might surprise me,' Alessio drawled in sardonic invitation.

Daisy paled. 'Oh, yes, I forgot... I'm such a shallow person, aren't I? I'd be wasting my breath telling you anything.'

As she attempted to brush past him, Alessio caught her arm in a powerful grip and yanked her back. 'No more running away,' he spelt out grimly.

'Let go of me!' Daisy blazed.

Instead he took her mouth in a hard, punishing kiss. Her world swung violently and dizzily on its axis, her legs buckling as his tongue stabbed between her lips in an expression of raw, hungry need. She struggled to resist and then surrendered as a river of fire ignited low in the pit of her stomach. With a moan of helpless response, burned by the ferocious heat of his desire, Daisy wrapped her arms round his throat.

'I'm still not speaking to you,' she mumbled shakily. 'I want you to know that.'

'I'm a jealous, possessive toad. We both know it. What is there to discuss?' Alessio demanded unevenly, divesting her of her bikini top and letting his hands rise to cup her bared breasts with a shameless groan of appreciation. '*Dio* ... I would burn a thousand years in purgatory for this alone!'

Crushing her to him, he lifted her high in his arms and carried her into the villa. 'The staff...?' she began.

'I sent them home.'

They landed on the bed in a wild tangle of damp limbs. Alessio pulled her over him, golden eyes smouldering over the pouting swell of pale breasts adorned by succulent pink nipples. Her breath was trapped in her throat as he stroked the painfully taut buds, sending shivers of excitement coursing through her.

'You are the only woman I have ever loved,' Alessio murmured roughly. 'And I want to be inside you so badly, I ache.'

As he reached up and played with the excruciatingly sensitive peaks with his teeth and his tongue, Daisy cried out, shifting briefly to bury her mouth hungrily in the hollow of his strong brown throat. Her worshipping hands travelled up over his broad chest, loving the flex of his muscles and the rough curls of black hair that met her exploring fingertips. He tangled his hands in her hair and dragged her lips back to his in an explosive kiss that melted her bones to hot honey. The sun-warmed scent and the never forgotten feel of him engulfed her, leaving her utterly without defence.

'*Yes!*' she gasped as he forced her down to him again and the hard, smooth jut of his manhood pressed against her belly, extracting a whimper of urgent, breathless need from her.

She couldn't get enough of him. She couldn't get close enough to satisfy herself. He rolled over, an impatient hand skimming the clinging bikini pants from her slender hips. Her heartbeat thundered as he found the pale, damp curls at the junction of her thighs and moved onto discover the hot, silken flesh she opened to him. And then, as suddenly, she could hardly get breath into her lungs and what she could burned and rasped in her throat as sensation clawed at her with a bitter-sweet intensity that was more than she could bear.

As he explored the aching, wet emptiness at the very heart of her, a long, sobbing moan of tormented frustration was dragged from Daisy. Never in her life had she craved anything as much as she craved the hot, hard invasion of Alessio's body into hers. She clutched at him with wildly impatient, pleading hands, out of control, drawing her knees back in feverish invitation.

Alessio lifted her up to him, eyes ablaze with answering desire, and entered her with a single powerful thrust. A startled cry of pain escaped her as intimate muscles locked tight in instinctive rejection.

Alessio stilled in shock. Astonished golden eyes raked her hotly flushed face. '*Dio* ... you feel as tight as the first time we made love!'

Ungritting her teeth, Daisy looked up at him.

'Like a virgin,' Alessio breathed in hoarse, shaken addition. 'I hurt you.'

But the pain had already receded and her wildly sensitive flesh was now aware of his intrusion on a very different plane. Her eyes slid shut in voluptuous acceptance. She gave a sensuous little wriggle, excitement taking hold of her again. He felt so incredibly good inside her, filling her, stretching her.

'Just how long has it been since you made love?' Alessio demanded unevenly.

'Please...' she moaned, every fibre of her straining body maddened by the stillness of his.

'How long?' Alessio grated with all the persistence of a natural-born torturer.

'Thirteen years!' Daisy shot at him in a burst of anguished frustration.

'Madre di Dio, piccola mia...' Alessio growled in a daze of disbelief.

He studied her with stunned intensity, a dark surge of blood rising to highlight his cheekbones, his shimmering eyes clinging to hers. And then, with a driven groan, he sank into her, deepening his penetration with fiery dominance. He delved his tongue between her lips with a sense of erotic timing that made every nerve-ending scream. There was only him then, and the incredible intensity of what he was making her feel.

He drove into her hard and fast. She rode a storm of frantic, feverish excitement, her heart slamming wildly against her breastbone. Then, without warning, the excruciating ache inside her intensified sharply, making her sob out his name in torment. A split second later, the wildness inside her expanded in a blazing explosion of sensation, shooting a hot, sweet overload of pleasure into every quivering inch of her being.

Alessio shuddered in the clinging circle of her arms and with a shout of hoarse, agonised satisfaction he found his own release, collapsing down on top of her, heavy and damp with sweat and achingly familiar. A raw flood of tenderness filled Daisy to overflowing and made her eyes smart. But he had finally got the truth out of her—a truth she had never dreamt she might speak or he might suspect—and now she felt naked and horribly exposed.

'You were worth waiting for,' Daisy whispered tightly, painfully.

Alessio lifted his dark, tousled head. With a slightly unsteady hand he smoothed her silky hair from her brow, long, caressing fingers cradling her cheekbone in a gesture of almost awkward tenderness. Only then, disturbingly, his beautiful dark eyes slewed away from the anxious intensity of hers, his lush lashes screening his gaze, but not before she'd seen the daunting bleakness etched there.

'I feel bloody guilty,' he confessed, and immediately released her from his weight.

Daisy didn't know what she had expected from him but it hadn't been that admission.

'Why no one else in all this time?' Alessio prompted tautly.

Now, that question was predictable but not one which Daisy was prepared to answer honestly. Defensively she turned her head away, aching with love for him and suppressing a dangerous urge to close the physical gap he had opened up between them. 'When you have to look at a man and think, How would I feel if I got pregnant by him? it kind of chills your bones.'

Instead of laughing as she had hoped, Alessio sat up in a sudden movement and swore long and low in Italian. '*Porca miseria*,' he finally groaned. 'I didn't *use* anything!'

Daisy lay with all the life of a block of wood. His horror at that realisation had the same effect on her as several blows with a hatchet.

'Don't you understand?' Alessio gritted, as if he was expecting more of a reaction from her. 'I didn't take any precautions!'

'Relax,' Daisy urged in a choky little voice. 'I doubt if I'm as fertile as I was at seventeen.'

'*Dio* . . . what have I done?' he bit out, only half under his breath.

Daisy hunched herself under the cover of the sheet. Witnessing Alessio's appalled response to the risk that he might have fathered a child with her a second time was, she was convinced, the most humiliating and painful dose of hard reality that she had ever experienced. Hurt and bitter tears boiled up behind her lowered eyelids.

'I feel incredibly guilty,' Alessio said again.

'Go away,' Daisy mumbled thickly, not even caring what he might have to feel guilty about any more.

A surprisingly hesitant hand came down on her rigid shoulder. She shook it off and scooted over to the far side of the bed. 'Leave me alone!'

His weight left the bed. But ironically she didn't want what she had said she wanted and immediately started feeling bereft and deserted and resentful.

'Get some sleep,' Alessio urged heavily. 'I have to go out for a while.'

'Don't come back,' Daisy spat, and burst into floods of tears the minute the door closed. She crammed her fist against her mouth but she still sobbed herself hoarse.

Obviously Alessio had no feelings for her other than lust. And now he clearly wished he hadn't bothered with that either. So why had he dragged her off to bed?

No doubt it had been part and parcel of his desire to put on a show of marital harmony for Tara's home-coming. Their daughter would undoubtedly not be impressed by the fact that the parents she wanted to regard as reunited lovers were sleeping in separate bedrooms.

CHAPTER TEN

DAISY was still in bed when the phone rang. At first she ignored it but the persistence of the caller finally triumphed and she reached for the receiver in a sudden spasm of irritation, no longer able to bear that intrusive shrill.

The feminine burst of imperious Italian reproof that greeted her was instantly recognisable. 'Bianca?' Daisy flatly broke into the flood of complaint. 'This is Daisy, not one of the staff. Alessio's out. Shall I ask him to call you?'

'Actually it was you I wanted to speak to,' Bianca informed her, her annoyance suddenly replaced by saccharine sweetness. 'I'm well aware that Alessio isn't at home. Shall I tell you *how* I know? He's with Nina...'

Daisy tensed and then slowly expelled her pent-up breath in a hiss. 'Don't you ever give up, Bianca? Thirteen years on, you're still playing the same old silly tune!'

'Check it out for yourself if you don't believe me! Nina is staying in a holiday complex only a few minutes' drive from the villa.' Bianca reeled off the address with audible satisfaction. 'Alessio's Ferrari is parked at the door—'

'You're wasting your time,' Daisy told her angrily. 'I'm not a credulous teenager any more and I trust Alessio...do you hear me? I trust your brother!'

'But you put him in an impossible position. Alessio wanted his daughter. He *had* to marry you! You're the intruder, not Nina!' Bianca condemned sharply. 'It's Nina he wants to be with and *is* with at this very moment! Why don't you get out of his life and leave him alone?'

Without hesitation, Daisy slammed the receiver back down on the cradle. She was shaking. Moisture beaded her short upper lip. In an abrupt movement, she sprang out of bed, knelt down, traced the phone wire to the wall and hurriedly disconnected it. It occurred to her that it would be nice if she could as easily disconnect the unsettling thoughts that kept assailing her no matter how hard she tried to block them out.

Why had Alessio behaved like a man suffering from a very uneasy conscience? Why had he twice said how guilty he felt? Daisy paced the carpet. As a rule, Alessio was outrageously stubborn and confident of his own judgement. Retreat was an unknown option to him and regret a rare emotion. But Alessio had been upset. That same scenario ran back and forth through her restive brain.

Alessio... appalled at the smallest risk that he might have made his wife pregnant. Why? Why *should* that be such a disaster? They were married. They were mature adults now. He adored Tara. He had admitted how very much he would have liked to share their daughter's early years. He did not dislike children. And surely the oddest thing of all was that he should have made no attempt to discover Daisy's feelings on the subject...

It was ridiculous even to *think* that he might be with Nina, Daisy scolded herself angrily. She had seen no evidence of questionable intimacy between Alessio and Nina the day before. Do you really think they would advertise if they planned to continue their affair in secret? a little voice asked drily. Indeed, hadn't the distinct lack of strain between them been in itself more suspicious?

Daisy pulled on a black cotton skirt and scoop-necked pink silk T-shirt. But she was not going out. No, definitely not. She would be waiting downstairs for Alessio when he came back. They had to talk, not least about Bianca. For heaven's sake, they had only been married a couple of days! On the other hand, wouldn't finding Alessio at that address be *her* proof that his sister had contacted her to tell her where he was? After all, how else would Daisy have been able to locate him?

Suddenly appreciating that she had a perfect excuse for checking out Bianca's story, Daisy did not hesitate. There was another car in the garage. It was bucketing down with rain but she didn't waste time running back indoors to get a coat. Driving out onto the road in the Mercedes, she told herself that it would be amusing to confront Alessio when he least expected her. And, whoever he was visiting in that complex, she was convinced it would not turn out to be Nina Franklin.

The Ferrari was sitting in a well-lit parking area. Daisy stopped on the other side of the road. As soon as she saw Alessio she would get out of the car. She didn't have long to wait. The door of a ground-floor apartment opened and a rectangle of light silhouetted Alessio's arrogant dark head and lean, powerful body. He was wearing his pearl-grey suit, the jacket open, his tie missing. Daisy slid out of the Mercedes.

And only then did she realise that Alessio wasn't alone. The door slammed noisily and Nina hurried down the path after him, calling out his name at the top of her voice. 'Alessio...!'

They walked together to the Ferrari, engaged in seemingly urgent conversation. Daisy stood and watched as they climbed into the car and drove off. Her legs felt as if they had turned to stone. She couldn't move. Rain soaked her hair, dripped down her face and drenched the silk T-shirt until it clung like a second skin to her chilled flesh. She didn't feel cold or wet. Shock had temporarily deprived her of sense and awareness.

And then a wave of sick dizziness ran over her and she shivered violently. She hadn't believed, she *truly* hadn't believed that he would be with Nina... that he could have made passionate love to her and then gone straight to another woman, a gorgeous, sophisticated blonde in her early twenties. No wonder he had an uneasy conscience...

The flood of pain which followed the disbelief hit Daisy on the drive back to the villa. He had to be in love with Nina. She could not believe that Alessio would betray her for anything less than love. In her mind, it all seemed so agonisingly clear. He *had* married her purely to get hold of Tara. He hadn't once pretended otherwise, had he? But evidently he had never expected their marriage to last indefinitely.

The break would have come once Tara was settled in Italy. Alessio would have waited until his daughter had forged closer ties with his half of the family. He had married her to *steal* their daughter, Daisy thought, in an agony of grief and betrayal. Setting out to win her trust, he had no doubt planned to ditch her as soon as she became surplus to requirements. Meanwhile he could continue to meet up with Nina whenever he liked.

'If it is the last thing I do in this lifetime, I will punish you for this,' Alessio had sworn the very day he had found out that he was a father. How could she have allowed herself to forget that threat?

Tears streaming down her face, Daisy stumbled back into the villa, fighting to regain control of emotions which felt uncontrollable. Dully she wondered why

Alessio had behaved as if he was jealous when surely he should not have cared less how she had lived in the years they had been apart. Maybe it had been a kind of crazy dog-in-the-manger possessiveness. Or maybe...just maybe he had seen the error of his ways and had raced off to see Nina tonight to break off that relationship. But then why would Nina have got into the Ferrari with him? she asked herself, ashamed of her eagerness to grasp at any explanation which might lessen the anguish of what she was feeling.

'Daisy?' a hatefully familiar voice murmured smoothly.

Daisy jerked and swivelled round. Strolling out of the drawing room with all the confidence of the mistress of the house, Bianca surveyed her and smiled with unconcealed satisfaction.

'You look like a drowned rat,' Bianca commented drily. 'I gather you hit pay dirt and, of course, you can't possibly want to be here when Alessio returns.'

With an immense effort, Daisy straightened her slight shoulders and walked past the sneering brunette into the drawing room. Her legs were trembling beneath her. But it demanded even greater discipline not to lay violent hands upon Bianca and throw her physically from the door of her brother's house. Bianca was here to gloat; she simply had been unable to resist the temptation to have a firsthand view of Daisy's devastation.

With an unsteady hand, Daisy reached for the brandy decanter and began pouring herself a drink, praying that alcohol would ward off the disorienting effect of shock and lessen the freezing coldness settling into her bones. 'I want you to leave,' she said without even sparing a glance at the other woman.

'Don't be childish,' Bianca urged impatiently.

'And before you leave I would like you to return your keys to this house. Now that your brother is married, I don't think it's appropriate for you to be walking in without warning whenever the fancy takes you,' Daisy completed before she braced herself and drank down the brandy all in one go, trembling as the heat raced down her aching throat and warmed the chilled pit of her uneasy stomach.

Bianca stared at Daisy, a faint hint of disconcertion drawing her brows together. 'I'm willing to drive you to the airport,' she announced, loftily ignoring the invitation to depart. 'You're obviously in no fit state to get yourself there!'

The airport. It would be so easy to take advantage of that invitation to run away. Indeed such a speedy retreat from a painful crisis would have all the ease and familiarity of habit, Daisy conceded painfully, drawing in a deep, shuddering breath to steady herself. However, she had Tara's feelings to consider. In addition, strange as it might seem, she wanted—no, she *needed* to confront Alessio this time. 'I don't require a lift to the airport, Bianca.'

'There's only one more flight to London tonight,' the brunette warned sharply. 'You haven't got much time.'

'I have all the time in the world,' Daisy countered tightly, frowning as a faint sound from somewhere beyond the room momentarily pierced her concentration. She focused briefly on the ajar door, listening for a split second before turning back to Bianca. 'I have all the time in the world,' she repeated with conviction, 'because I'm not going anywhere.'

Bianca studied her in contemptuous disbelief. 'You can't be serious! You can't want to be here when Alessio gets back. How could you want to humiliate yourself to that extent? If I caught my husband in the act of an adulterous tryst with another woman, believe me, I wouldn't be sitting humbly waiting for him to come home again!'

Daisy was rigid, her pallor pronounced. 'But then what I do... and indeed what Alessio does... is none of your business, Bianca. You're his sister, not his keeper.'

'Alessio and I are very close!' Bianca shot back at her in angry resentment. 'And I want you out of his life for good!'

Daisy uttered a strangled laugh. 'The same way you wanted rid of me the last time? You lied about Sophia Corsini and I swallowed your every lie whole,' she condemned, bitter resentment flooding through her. 'He never even went out with the wretched girl!'

Bianca flushed and then her jawline hardened, her mouth thinning as she made a recovery. 'Where on earth did you get the idea that I lied about Sophia? Alessio may be my brother but even I have never tried to pretend that he's the faithful type—'

'I'm sick of listening to your poison,' Daisy interrupted fiercely.

'You just haven't got the courage to face the truth. If you had any pride at all, you would be getting out before Alessio makes an even bigger fool of you! He doesn't want you; he *never* wanted you!' Bianca asserted in furious frustration. 'All he ever wanted was his daughter! How can you try to cling to him even after I've given you the proof that he's still involved with Nina!'

Without warning the door was thrust back noisily on its hinges.

Both Daisy and Bianca jumped, their heads spinning in unison. Alessio stood on the threshold, diamond-hard eyes blazing with outrage, his golden skin pale with anger.

'Nina is waiting for you at her apartment, Bianca,' Alessio breathed with chilling bite. 'She's most unhappy with the dramatic role you have assigned to her. She doesn't appreciate being used as a weapon—'

'I don't know what you're talking about!' Bianca broke in, a mottled flush overlying her tautened cheeks.

'Spurred on by you, Nina had no objection to causing a little minor mischief, but she draws the line at setting out to destroy my marriage. She's already ashamed of the lies you instructed her to tell yesterday. You misjudged your partner, Bianca.' Alessio's grim gaze rested on his sister in harsh condemnation, his nostrils flaring with distaste. 'She thinks your malicious games have got dangerously out of control . . . and, believe me, she's not the only one!'

Every scrap of colour had now drained from Bianca's complexion. She stared at her brother in mingled shock and embarrassment. 'Alessio, you don't understand,' she began shakily. 'I was only thinking of your happiness.'

Alessio crossed the floor, closed a determined hand round his twin's elbow and practically dragged her out of the room with him.

Daisy's knees wouldn't hold her up any longer. She sagged down like a broken doll onto the nearest seat. From the hall, staccato Italian broke from Alessio, scorching anger powering every syllable, Bianca's responses running from defensive to pleading to—finally—tearful. Throughout, Daisy's temples pounded with tension. She couldn't yet think straight but she could not miss hearing the resounding slam of the front door as Alessio saw his sister off the premises.

'You're soaking wet, *piccola mia*...' Alessio gritted, crouching down until he was on a level with her, his vibrantly handsome features still dark and taut with fury, although there was a curious tenderness that bewildered her in the golden eyes that rested on her strained face. 'You need to get out of those clothes before you catch pneumonia.'

Stiff as a little clockwork soldier, Daisy cloaked her gaze in self-defence. Springing upright, Alessio swooped down on her again and swept her up into his arms without another word. A startled gasp burst from Daisy. She was not in the mood to be soothed like a distressed child.

'Nina wants to apologise to you but I told her that this wasn't the right time.'

'Apologise...she wants to *apologise*?' Daisy pressed in disbelief. 'Alessio, if you don't put.me down I'll scream!'

In response to her challenge, Alessio merely tightened his arms round her as he started up the stairs. 'Daisy...my relationship with Nina was never anything but casual. A prudent male thinks twice before he becomes intimately involved with the daughter of family friends.' Thrusting back their bedroom door, he murmured grimly, 'Nina's ego was hurt when I married you and Bianca found her an easy target. But Nina, spoilt and self-centred as she is, has a conscience—'

'I didn't notice it yesterday when she was blowing kisses at you and spouting all that nonsense about Barry!' Daisy retorted, tearing herself violently free of his hold as soon as he began to lower her to the bathroom carpet. 'And I don't know what kind of a story you've invented as a cover-up but it won't wash because I wasn't born yesterday! You were *with* Nina tonight!'

'Bianca is staying with her. That's why I went over there. I phoned before I left but when I arrived Bianca had gone,' Alessio explained with an impatient frown, his brilliant eyes assessing Daisy's now flushed and furious face. 'When I confronted Nina, she was very upset—'

'And only yesterday you told me that she was behaving *so* generously!'

At that tart reminder, faint colour accentuated the taut slant of Alessio's hard cheekbones. 'I was feeling uncomfortable because I dropped Nina the minute you came back into my life. Yesterday, I genuinely couldn't see the wood for the trees, but I was furious with her tonight—'

'Is that why you tucked her into your Ferrari with you?' Daisy prompted in a tone of fierce accusation.

'So that's why you're wet.' Alessio surveyed her with dawning comprehension. 'You *followed* me?'

Her cheeks burning but her chin angled high, Daisy told him about his sister's phone call.

Alessio vented a sharp imprecation. 'I was determined to find Bianca, and Nina thought she knew where she was. When we drew a blank, I dropped Nina straight back home again. If you saw us together, surely you noticed that she was crying?'

'Sorry, I forgot my binoculars. Now go away. I want a bath,' Daisy announced brittly.

Alessio studied her, his golden eyes incredulous. '*Dio* . . . in the midst of all this?'

Daisy planted a determined hand on his chest, pressed him back and slammed the door in his face. But the instant she was alone she slumped, the anger she had forced to the fore in self-defence draining away. She had gone on the attack sooner than let Alessio see how pitifully fragile her self-control was.

So, Alessio had finally become suspicious and, setting out to confront his sister, had ended up dealing with Nina first. Intense relief washed over Daisy as she tasted the truth. Bianca had been telling a pack of lies and now that Alessio was aware of his twin's venomous loathing for his wife Bianca would never be in a position to cause trouble again.

Shivering now with cold, she ripped off her sodden clothing and stepped into a shallow bath. But her sense of relief was short-lived. Misery invaded her afresh. Nothing had really changed between them, she thought wretchedly. Alessio might not be in love with Nina but he didn't love her either. And he had reacted to the possibility of another baby in the same way that he might have reacted to a death threat. She couldn't even cherish the hope that extending the family might help to bring them closer.

The door opened.

Daisy tensed, feeling hunted. *'What?'* she demanded.

'You have a count of three to vacate that bath,' Alessio murmured dangerously softly. *'One—'*

'I'm staying put!'

'Two—'

'You're turning into a domineering tyrant!' Daisy screeched, nearly falling out of the bath in her haste to snatch up a towel.

She emerged from the bathroom with pronounced reluctance. Alessio was lounging back against the footboard of the bed. He rested diamond-bright eyes on her hotly flushed and mutinous face. 'When you were with Bianca, you made a reference to a girl called Sophia...'

Daisy paled and chewed her lower lip. 'Thirteen years ago, Bianca told me that Sophia had been your girlfriend and that you were seeing her again—'

'*Madre di Dio* ... no longer do I need to wonder why you agreed to the divorce!' Alessio bit out rawly.

'At the time it seemed to make sense,' Daisy muttered ruefully.

'*Porca miseria* ... the damage Bianca has caused! I never dreamt that she could be such a bitch!'

'But then she doesn't behave like that with you,' Daisy sighed.

'She made that call to Barry Stevens...' A bitter tension had hardened Alessio's strong features and roughened his deep voice. 'I'm sorry that you have had to endure her malicious attacks, even sorrier that I refused to listen when you tried to tell me what was happening!'

He was still appalled and mortified by his sister's behaviour. Daisy was struggling to overcome a powerfully embarrassing urge to wrap consoling arms around him. Any move to offer comfort would be uniquely revealing to a male as shrewd as Alessio. And Daisy was not prepared to tell him that in spite of everything she loved him even more than she had loved him as a teenager. Only this time she wouldn't run away—she would stay and fight, if need be, to give their marriage a future.

'I'm not blaming you for what Bianca did. It's over and done with. Forget about it,' she urged in a rush.

'That's very forgiving of you,' Alessio murmured tautly.

A thunderous silence stretched.

Alessio strode restively over to the window. Then he swung fluidly back to face her, expelling his breath in a hiss. 'I've been acting like an insanely jealous and irrational teenager ever since I saw those photo albums of yours,' he admitted in a driven undertone. 'When I found out today that . . . well, that there had never been anyone else I was really ashamed of my behaviour. I had no right whatsoever to question your past.'

Daisy rubbed abstractedly at the deep-pile carpet with a set of bare pink toes. 'I've always been pretty possessive about you too,' she muttered.

Alessio threw back his darkly handsome head, his brilliant eyes bleak. 'I wouldn't have acted like that if I hadn't been so afraid of losing you again,' he gritted.

'I thought it was Tara you were afraid of losing,' Daisy whispered slowly.

'Much as I love our daughter, *piccola mia*, I have to confess that I used her as an excuse to make you marry me again. I was a man with a mission last week,' Alessio grated unevenly. 'And my mission was to win, by any means within my power, a second chance with the girl I loved and lost as a teenager. If I had only wanted Tara I would never have forced you into marriage.'

Daisy's violet eyes were wide. With immense difficulty she relocated her voice. 'But you kept on *telling* me that it was all for Tara's sake!'

'That was pride talking. *Madre di Dio . . .*' Alessio groaned. 'You fell apart in horror when I first mentioned marriage! So I cornered you and blackmailed you into it—'

'You bought the agency because you wanted me back,' Daisy mumbled dizzily, struggling to conceal her delight.

'I thought if I pushed hard enough I could somehow make you feel what I was feeling,' Alessio confessed roughly. 'That first day I saw you again, it was like coming alive for the first time in thirteen years! *Dio . . .* I had your phone number within an hour of you leaving me again!' Crossing the room with a look of fierce decisiveness stamped on his taut features, he reached for her with determined hands. Dark golden eyes blazed down at her. 'This marriage *can* work. I love you enough for both of us!'

Daisy braced shaking hands on his broad shoulders, her throat closing over. 'Alessio,' she said thickly, 'I love you too.'

He stared down at her fixedly.

Daisy swallowed convulsively. 'I never stopped loving you but I thought you only wanted Tara and I was so scared of getting hurt again.'

With a stifled groan, Alessio crushed her to him, snatching her up off her feet to plunder her readily parted lips with an aching, desperate hunger every bit as strong as her own as he brought her down to the bed. Intense happiness and excitement swept Daisy to a breathless height of emotion that drove every other thought from her mind.

Leaning over her, Alessio curved a possessive palm round one delicate cheekbone, his fingers lacing gently into her hair as he studied her with wondering, mesmeric intensity.

Then, disturbingly, his strong face shadowed. 'I still feel so damned guilty about this afternoon,' he confided heavily. '*Dio* . . . I was crazy with the need to make love to you but there is no excuse for that kind of carelessness. If I've made you pregnant again, you're going to hate me!'

Daisy focused on him in bewilderment. 'Hate you?'

'You were so miserable when you were carrying Tara,' Alessio said tensely. 'I know that having another baby is completely out of the question and I'd never ask you to go through all that again for my benefit, but—'

'You said you didn't want another child because you assumed that that was what *I* wanted to hear...' A breathtaking smile slowly blossomed on Daisy's face as she made that leap in understanding. 'But there were a whole host of things wrong between us then... Now that everything's right... actually... I'd love another baby.'

Alessio looked stunned. For a count of ten seconds he simply stared at her. Daisy grinned, enjoying the knowledge that for once he had not been one step ahead of her. 'I mean *this* time I could really enjoy the experience,' she pointed out chattily...

Sheathed in a diaphanous negligé set, Daisy strolled in from the balcony and watched Alessio pulling on a pair of jeans. Next door to watching him take them off, it was one of her favourite pursuits. Every fluid movement of those long, bronzed, hair-roughened limbs utterly entranced her. Had it been a year, had it really been a whole year since they'd remarried?

She surveyed the elegant bedroom of their town house in Rome. After lunch, they would be driving down to the villa for the weekend. Last night they had attended a surprise party thrown by Alessio's parents to celebrate their first wedding anniversary. The Leopardis had flown her aunt over for the festivities and Janet was staying with them for several days. Indeed even Bianca had put in a brief appearance and Daisy had ended up feeling a little sorry for her sister-in-law.

When Alessio had exposed Bianca's malicious lies, his sister had gone home to her parents for sympathy, only to find herself the target of yet another bout of outraged recriminations. Unhappily for her, it had not occurred to her that her parents were *genuinely* eager to see Alessio's marriage succeed or that they were overjoyed at the prospect of getting to know their grandchild. Finding herself and her opinions very much out in the cold, Bianca had cut herself off from her family for months.

However, last night Bianca had approached them with a small present and stilted congratulations, her discomfiture painfully apparent.

'We made it in spite of you,' Alessio had growled ungraciously, only accepting the present after Daisy had given him a speaking glance, but then adding, 'And do I need to remind you what people say about Greeks bearing gifts?'

Certainly it would be a long time before Alessio trusted his sister again.

'You look ravishing, *piccola mia . . .*'

Snatched from her reverie by that innately sexy voice, Daisy collided with Alessio's intensely appreciative gaze and blushed like a teenager. They had made love until dawn had broken the skies but her heart still skipped an impressionable beat.

'It's such a beautiful morning.' She had been out on the balcony reliving the sheer romance of the previous night when Alessio had presented her with a magnificent diamond eternity ring and informed her that this had been without doubt the very happiest year of his entire life.

Alessio closed possessive arms round her and pressed a whisper of a kiss to the sensitive skin at the nape of her neck. 'It's still early. How do you feel about breakfast in bed?' he murmured wickedly.

Taut with delicious tension, Daisy leant back against his hard length, and then a trio of knocks, loud enough to wake the dead, sounded on the door. Tara peered round the barrier with exaggerated care.

'Honestly, you two are the limit . . . it's only ten in the morning!' Emerging fully into view, Tara brandished a rather startlingly clad infant for their inspection. 'Nanny's doing the packing, so I got Jen dressed.'

Sinking down on the bed with a smile, Daisy opened her arms to receive her two-month-old daughter, Jenny. Soulful dark brown eyes looked up at her mother from below a virulent lime-green baseball cap.

'What's she wearing?' Alessio demanded, apparently transfixed by the garish lime, purple and orange miniature dungarees.

'Dad, if I have a sister fourteen years younger, it helps if she's got street cred. Take it from me, this is what the cool baby is wearing this season . . . not those disgusting embroidered dresses with those weird frilly socks which Mum loves. I took pity on Jen when I was out shopping with my friends yesterday.'

'That was very thoughtful of you.' Daisy tried not to laugh as Alessio came down beside her, deftly stole Jenny from her lap and gently lifted the baseball cap in the hope of finding his youngest daughter's tiny face.

Alessio's gaze briefly met Daisy's in a shared instant of vibrant amusement as they watched Tara prowl round the room, eye-catching as a bird of paradise in colours that were a remarkable match for her baby sister's. Their daughter was chattering at length about her plans for the family's amusement over the weekend. And they *were* a family, Daisy reflected, a soft sigh of unvarnished contentment escaping her.

Alessio had spent the past year showing her in a thousand different ways just how much he loved her and valued their marriage. Her pregnancy had been a time of real happiness for all of them. Alessio and Tara had both been thrilled to bits and Daisy had been as cosseted as a precious piece of highly breakable china. Jenny had been born a week early and with the bare minimum of fuss. With the assistance of a sensible English nanny, Daisy was thoroughly enjoying motherhood the second time around.

Tara had settled into school, made plenty of new friends and now spoke Italian with enviable fluency. Her outgoing, confident personality had eased her passage everywhere. Her grandparents adored her, and though in the early months of her move to Italy their indulgence had led to Alessio and his daughter having several tussles for supremacy Tara now had a healthy respect for her father and his rules.

'Right,' Tara said bossily as she bent down and scooped her baby sister away from the combined attentions of her besotted parents. 'Jen needs her nap now. We don't want her being all cross and cranky on the drive down, do we? You two don't need to hurry downstairs—'

'We *don't*?' Daisy echoed in surprise.

'Of course not. Lunch is hours away and even Janet's still in bed,' Tara acknowledged carelessly as she made for the door again. 'You know, three is a nice round number...'

'I beg your pardon?' Daisy frowned.

Tara popped her head back round the door, an impish smile on her mobile features. 'That means you can return to what you were doing when I came in. I'm putting in an order for a little brother. As babies go, Jen's really cute, but she needs company in her own age group.'

'Jenny's only ten weeks old!' Daisy gasped as the door shut.

A vibrant smile curving his sensual mouth, Alessio lowered his dark head to hers again, wolfish amusement glittering in his intent gaze. He closed two gentle hands round Daisy's slight shoulders and slowly pressed her back on the pillows. 'As an excuse to spend a great deal of time in bed, the idea has incredible appeal,' he confessed with husky satisfaction.

'I'll consider it...in about six months,' Daisy muttered breathlessly, drowning in his dark golden gaze.

'*Dio, piccola mia,* I love you so much; how did I ever survive thirteen years without you?'

Daisy ran a possessive set of fingers along a long, lean male thigh temptingly and invitingly clad in taut denim. 'I love you too,' she sighed. 'You put your jeans on just so that I could take them off again...'

HARLEQUIN ◆ PRESENTS®

Coming soon...

June 1997—Long Night's Loving (#1887)

by Anne Mather

New York Times bestselling author,
with over 60 million books in print

"Pleasure for her readers." —*Romantic Times*

and

July 1997—A Haunting Obsession (#1893)

by Miranda Lee

one of Presents' brightest stars,
with over 10 million books sold worldwide

"Superb storytelling." —*Romantic Times*

Top author treats from Harlequin Presents.
Make this summer the hottest ever!